FAKE FRIENDS
A NEVER JUST FRIENDS NOVEL

Copyright ©

FAKE FRIENDS - 2020 Saxon James

All rights reserved.

First published in Australia by May Books 2020

Newcastle, NSW, Australia

No parts of this publication may be reproduced, stored in a retrieval system, or transmitted in any form or by any means, electronic, mechanical, photocopying, recording, or otherwise, without the prior written permission of the copyright owner.

This book is sold subject to the condition that it shall not, by way of trade or otherwise, be lent, resold, hired out, or otherwise circulated without the publisher's prior consent in any form of binding or cover other than that in which it is published and without a similar condition including this condition being imposed on the subsequent purchaser. Under no circumstances may any part of this book be photocopied for resale.

This is a work of fiction. Any similarity between the characters and situations within its pages and places or persons, living or dead, is unintentional and co-incidental.

To anyone who's ever had to fake it.

SAXON JAMES

FAKE FRIENDS
A NEVER JUST FRIENDS NOVEL

Saxon James

FAKE FRIENDS

CHAPTER ONE
CIRCUS

There comes a time in every man's life where he has to choose which of his friends to give twenty-five thousand dollars.

And more importantly, which of them looks best in a swimsuit.

I take a sip of my beer and push the offer to the back of my mind. There's still a week until *Royal Swimwear* wants a response, and while the money means sweet fuck all to me, Royce and Tanner could probably put it to good use.

Royce is smiling across the table like a goddamn idiot, which only makes me laugh. For someone who's usually so guarded and straight-faced, he's been walking on clouds since he and Tanner got together.

I lift my glass. "Congrats again, guys. If anyone can turn that filthy shack into a home, it's you two."

My best friend, Leon, knocks his glass against mine, and Jules giggles.

The last few weeks, I've been coming into town less and less, and I'm a bit worried I'm sinking back into that reclusive side of me that comes out when I need to hide from the world. So tonight has been nice. Celebrating Royce and Tanner buying their house together actually makes me happy. Because they're happy.

Drinks and deep-fried mozzarella sticks with my best friends in the world. Who the hell could feel down after that?

If I say it enough times I might convince myself.

Leon nudges his elbow into my side. "What are you thinking about?"

"Nothing."

"Bullshit. I know that look."

"Then you know there's nothing wrong." I force a big smile his way, which does nothing to dissolve his concerned expression. Not that I can blame him. I haven't seen Leon since the Sunflora Festival two weeks ago, and we never let that long pass without catching up.

"I saw Rowan Harvey the other day."

My back immediately stiffens at the name. Instinctively, I *know* Leon has pegged what's wrong, but I sure as hell wasn't expecting him to call me on it. "That's awesome news. I'm so happy for you."

"Cut the shit, Circus. Why is he back?"

"Why don't you ask him? Then we'll both know. Or, better still, let's just go on pretending that asshole doesn't exist and continue to live our lives in peace." My voice comes out a whole lot happier than I feel.

"I can strongly suggest he leaves town again."

"No need, I already made my thoughts very clear."

"Circus ..."

"How about we skip this conversation?" I drop the happy act. "We're here to celebrate, so why don't we just do that?" I raise my voice. "Who wants another round?"

I slide from the booth before anyone can comment and head for the long bar where I place an order for drinks. I add another platter of wings and mozzarella sticks to my bill, thinking that while they cook, it'll give me a few minutes away from everyone, where I can force Rowan Harvey back out of my mind.

Knowing he's in town, over five years since I last saw him, has had me on edge. It's why I've preferred to stay hidden away at home these last few weeks, too far out for anyone to find me.

And yet, I've been glancing at the doors all night. The Ugly Mug is the only bar in town, and other than driving over to Port Welling, there's not much else to do on a Saturday night in Sunbury. I've been expecting Rowan to walk in at any second, and the thought fills me with so much anger, I'm about to work myself into an ulcer.

I remind myself, again, that Rowan is firmly in the past and has nothing to do with me now.

I fish my phone out of my pocket and immediately the anxiety starts to settle. Social media is the ultimate distractor, and whenever I'm feeling down, or thinking too much about the past, it has a way of lightening my mood. There's a fair few notifications waiting, but when I click over to the photo I posted earlier, of me in the garden, overlooking the rocky face of Crown Trails, shaggy hair a mess in the wind, my gut sinks.

Less than a thousand interactions.

My second post in as many weeks that hasn't even broken four figures.

The urge to panic floods my mouth with a bitter taste, and I hurry to click back on the comments.

Circus is life
Ily please marry me
It's my birthday can you say hi?
Omigod PERFECTION
Splash emoji
Heart eyes emoji
Love heart and eggplant emojis

Each comment fuels my need to be loved, and I store their words away in my subconscious as I tap the Delete icon, and the failure of a post disappears from memory.

I'll do better tomorrow.

But even as I think that, I know I need more. All the other influencers that started around the same time as me have coupled up, and it's sent their popularity through the roof. I'm sure that's what *Royal Swimwear* is hoping will happen with me, which is why they set the stipulation of having two models in these shots.

I can't say I hate the idea.

It'd be nice to have a friend I could share that side of my life with, but that would also come with admitting that I take pretty pictures for a living when they're all out there working real jobs. And I need their respect like I need air. Like I need my followers. Like I need to pretend that just for one person, I'm the most important guy in their world.

The way I used to be for my parents.

And nope, not going there.

There's only one day a year I let myself be a total train wreck over them, and that day is coming up soon enough.

"Hey." I knock on the bar top to get Reynolds's attention. "I'll take those drinks over now." Because torn between Leon's questioning over Rowan or thinking about my dead parents, I know which topic I'd rather cover.

Only once I dump the drinks on the table and head back for the bar, I'm suddenly rethinking that choice. Because Rowan Harvey is standing there, clearly waiting for me.

He's leaning his elbows back on the counter, tattooed fingers linked over his stomach and blue eyes watching me steadily.

My heart does the familiar squeeze it's so well practiced at, and any other night, I might have been able to ignore his presence, but tonight, I'm already too raw.

So I turn on my heel and flee.

I'm out the doors and into the cool spring air before I'm pretty sure anyone has noticed I've left. My bike is propped up against the brick wall of the building, exactly where I left it because in a town like Sunbury, no one is going to steal your shit.

I stagger as I throw a leg over, and then it takes two attempts before my foot finds the pedal. Huh. So apparently I'm a tad drunk.

I start to laugh as I push the bike forward and struggle to hold the handlebars straight.

"You didn't have to run out on my account."

My head jerks up.

If hearing his name is enough to make my back tense, hearing his voice is enough to put every muscle in my body on guard.

"I haven't seen you around," he continues.

"No shit? Well, I'm sure that was really painful for you." Not as painful as, say, seeing the man who betrayed you five years ago and ran off before you could get the taste of his cum out of your mouth.

"Circus, come on, I just want to talk."

"Sorry, I don't do that anymore."

"*Talk?*"

"Give you my time." I push off and finally get my bike moving in the *forward* direction, but when Rowan falls into step beside me, I realize I'm possibly going *slower* on this thing than if I were walking.

"Can you just hear me out?"

"Hard no." My bike gives a solid wobble, but I correct it in time.

"Is it safe for you to be riding that thing right now?"

"Is it safe for me to be alone with you right now?"

"Circus, I—"

I ring my bell, obnoxiously loud in the quiet street, and cut off his words.

"Circus—"

I ring it again.

Then before I even see him move, Rowan steps into the street, and his hand closes over mine.

I jolt back like I've been shocked, and in all fairness, I think that's what happened. I *am* in shock. Shock over his closeness, his warmth, his presence.

And oh hell fucking no, motherfucker. My dick has apparently gone batshit crazy because it starts to perk up.

Doesn't it remember the last time it got all excited over him?

I stumble as I climb off my bike, and Rowan's left standing there holding it.

"All I want is for you to accept my apology," he begs. "Then I'll be gone again. I swear it."

"Aww." I cock my head in fake sympathy. "I guess you'll be here a while, then."

I make the mistake of meeting his eyes, and all those years we spent together hurl back through my memories. He steps forward. There's barely room for my bike between us. This close, it's easy to see all the ways he's grown up.

And the torn look on his face tells me all the ways he

hasn't.

I'd put money down that his closet door is still locked tight.

"Please, Kelly ..."

My real name snaps me out of whatever that was and sets my anger to red hot. "Don't you fucking dare."

"But—"

I yank my bike from his grip, and this time I get on it first go. The rage is burning through my drunkenness, and all I need is to put as much distance as possible between us. "You have no right to that name. You have no right to my forgiveness. Now get the hell out of my life." I push off and have enough coordination to get the bike moving a bit faster. "And this time, stay there."

CHAPTER TWO
ROWAN

Well, that could have gone better.

I've been waiting for weeks for Circus to show up in town again, so when I got a call from my sister to say he was at Ugly's, I'd gone straight down ...

And completely screwed my chance of getting a resolution.

Drinking myself into oblivion after he left probably wasn't the smartest choice either.

Oh well, it's another day.

I set about working the grill at Harvey's Burger House. While the diner has been in my family for years, I *do not* miss this part of Sunbury. It's hot work, and I swear by the end of every shift, my hands reek of onion and pickles.

It's a familiar smell from the year I spent working here between graduating high school and starting college.

"How are you doing?" Mom asks, leaving the office to check the orders.

"Yeah, fine. Not too busy."

She gives me her warm, motherly smile that never

fails to make me feel guilty. "I tell you, I'm glad you're back. Every time I see you out here again, it's like you never left."

I chuckle even though I'm not feeling it. "I was gone for five years." And I don't think I've ever spent five years more confused and lost than during my time in Portland. Being back here feels like I get another chance to start over. To forget the dumb choices I made in Portland and pick up my life where I left off.

I just wish it were that easy.

"Okay, well, before I start getting all sentimental that my boy is home ..." She takes a deep breath and pushes off the counter she was leaning against. "I've got some orders to place. Shout out if you need a hand, okay?"

"Will do."

She disappears back into the office, and my shoulders slump. Whenever I'm around my family, I always feel the need to be "on," and after only a month back here, I'm already exhausted by it.

The door to out front slams open, and my sister Piper rushes into the kitchen.

"Quick, we're swapping."

"We're doing what now?"

But Piper doesn't answer. She's already tugging off my apron and pushing me toward the door.

"Wait, no, stop." I laugh and grab her bony shoulders. It never occurred to me how much shorter she is until I spent some time away. "Calm it, sis. Explain."

"Circus is here," she hisses like it's some kind of secret.

And ... it sort of is. My gut does that thing where it turns into a storm-ravaged sea. I lick my lips and taste salt. "What's your point?"

"He *never* comes in here. Ever. And I have no idea why you have to talk to him, but now's your chance. Go."

She doesn't know. She could never. My sister is my biggest support, and I swear nothing I could do would ever make her think less of me, but ... what I did to Circus definitely toes that line.

Which is why I cannot talk to him about it here. This town is way too fucking nosy to discuss private business in my family's diner.

I force a smile as I take Piper's pad and pen. Yippee, go me. About to serve a guy who hates my guts. Seems like the perfect way to end the weekend.

And when I step out from behind the counter and see him sitting there, he steals my breath like always.

He's ... beautiful. There's no other way to describe him.

Circus has his mom's Italian skin and black hair, his dad's smoldering gray eyes. And I say "smoldering" not to sound like a complete douchebag, but because it's the most accurate way to describe them. They're always a little squinty, a little lustful, and they're what ultimately made me give in to every urge I'd been fighting for the better part of high school.

I swallow all that back and approach his table.

His relaxed expression immediately closes off as his eyes narrow, and I have to shift my attention from him to Royce.

"What can I get you guys?"

Royce lifts a sardonic eyebrow. "Since when do you do table service here?"

"You guys are just special, I guess."

"Uh-huh." He looks skeptical as hell, and it makes me wonder if Circus ever told him what happened between us. I always imagined he would run his mouth about me all over town—it was one of the reasons I took off—but when time passed with no whisper of it reaching my sister, I realized he'd somehow kept it to himself.

I don't deserve it.

But damn if I'm not grateful anyway.

From the corner of my eye, I notice Circus tuck his hands behind his head, lean arm muscles popping under his shirtsleeves, shaggy dark hair a sinful mess. I refuse to look.

Even as my mouth goes dry.

Even as I ache to touch.

I've managed to *mostly* ignore my craving for men for the past five years, but Circus has always had a way of breaking down my resolve.

"Have you guys decided?"

Royce nods and orders a black coffee with toast

before handing his menu to me. Then I have no choice but to look at Circus.

He's so ... laid-back now. I'm not used to the stillness. At school, he was always bouncing around and making people laugh, like he didn't have a care in the world. People used to call him a clown, but he figured, why be a clown when you can be the whole circus? It's where he got his name.

That person is clearly long gone now.

He watches me steadily, and it's like I can see fire brimming behind his eyes. I wouldn't be surprised if he's picturing punching *me* in the face.

"And you?"

"Granola and a green smoothie."

I frown. "Ah ... we don't do green smoothies. Just banana, strawberry, and chocolate."

He scoffs. "See, Royce? Told you we should have met at Peg's."

"Yeah, but Tanner and I always meet here. And you just *had* to talk to me this morning."

"I'm regretting that choice more and more each minute."

I'd say they've forgotten me as they bicker, but there's a tension crackling in the air between us that tells me Circus is just as aware of me as I am of him.

"Let me see what I can do," I eventually say, then leave them to it.

If Circus wants a dirty green drink, I'll get it for him.

If I have to be his personal waiter for a week—a *month!*—I'll do it.

Because no matter how much I tried to move on with my life in Portland, I couldn't do it.

Not after how I left things here.

I'd like to say that what I did to Circus was my only reason for running away, but my family played a big part in that decision too.

Especially my grandpa. And all the times he'd beaten "that sissy shit" out of me as a kid.

I let out a long breath.

Right. Green shit.

I google ingredients for a green smoothie and start to throw them together. It's not going to be what he's after, but it's the best I can do.

I grab Royce's coffee, and seeing Tanner walk in, I make his usual too. Then I head back to their table.

Circus's back is to me as I approach, and I catch the back end of the conversation. "... have a proposition for you."

Royce and Tanner share a look.

"Just hear me out," Circus continues. "It's super easy. All Royce would need to do is pose in this swimwear with me, plaster the pictures all over social media, and then he'll make an easy twenty-five K."

Twenty-five K? I almost drop the drinks, so I hurry to plonk them on the table. "That's a lot of money."

"Eavesdropping," Circus says. "What a complete

surprise."

"You're in a public place."

"And I wasn't talking to you." He picks up his smoothie, and I'm sure he wants another reason to throw a quip at me. But as he drinks, his eyes flick toward me, and then he hurries to set the glass on the table. I must have passed some kind of test because he stays quiet.

"What's going on here?" Tanner asks. "You guys were friends in high school. Did something happen?"

Only the worst moment of my entire life.

"Yeah," Circus replies. "I learned good judgment."

"What was this about photos?" I ask.

"What was this about minding your own goddamn business?" The forced civility in his tone is starting to slip. It makes my heartbeat kick up a notch.

And yes, he has every reason to hate me, but I need to remember the reasons for keeping my distance too. Namely, this insane pull I have to him.

"I still don't think I understand," Tanner says. "Someone wants to give you money to take photos in a swimsuit?"

"I'm an influencer," Circus explains. Which of course I already knew after stumbling across his social media account. "Brands give me money to wear their stuff so others will go buy it. But *Royals* wants someone to do it with me. They want it to be, ah, sexy."

Somehow I can just tell he's trying not to look at me.

Tanner reels back. "And you wanna get sexy with

Roo?"

For some reason Circus finds that hilarious, and I'm honestly surprised he hasn't told me to piss off yet.

"It's all an illusion. But I know Royce's freckles will get people's attention and make the shots stand out. I'd be happy to do it with you too, but can you honestly say you wouldn't be awkward as fuck, pressed up against me in only a swimsuit?"

Poor Tanner's whole face goes red. "Ah, no, definitely not. That's not for me."

Royce lifts a hand. "With all the love in the world, you don't have a chance in hell of me doing it either."

"It's over twenty grand!" I can't believe my ears.

Tanner shrugs. "Our mortgage isn't huge, and I'm not really about money. And it's not something Roo's ever had to worry about."

I will never understand not being motivated by money. It's just ... unnatural. "I'll do it." The words fall out of my mouth before I'm even sure what I'd do with them.

Circus snorts. "No, you won't."

"It's *twenty-five thousand dollars*. I would do just about anything for that kind of money."

He turns a blank expression on me. "*Including* punching someone in the face? Oh, wait, no. You do that for free."

The excitement that had been building slowly shrivels up. Thinking for even one second that he'd consider doing anything like that with me was stupid. I'm pretty sure Circus would rather give up the contract completely than let me at that kind of money.

And *damn*, it's a lot of money.

With that kind of cash, I could get out from under my family and actually do something *I* want to do. I could leave this stupid diner behind.

But ... that's never going to happen.

I let my disappointment sink in and give him a dry smile. "Just think about it."

Then I storm back out into the kitchen, relieve Piper of my apron, and get back to grilling burgers.

Because that is where someone like me belongs.

Just ask my grandpa. He'd say I'm atoning for my sinful thoughts, and dear *God,* Circus makes me have sinful thoughts.

I remember that night, five years ago. Even though I graduated the year before Circus, I still spent most of my free time with him, was addicted to him. And after seeing Circus leave Harvey's with his date earlier that night, I couldn't fight it anymore.

I remember how I snuck into his prom and stole him away into the back halls of the school. How I finally gave in and took the kiss I'd been dying to take for years. How Circus got on his knees and showed me what true pleasure is.

And where, in my post-orgasm high, one of my friends found us.

I'd pushed Circus up against the lockers and punched him clean in the face.

I grit my teeth against the tears that want to fall again and remind myself I don't deserve to let out even one.

I'm a piece of shit, and those kinds of thoughts bring nothing but trouble.

I just need Circus to forgive me so I can move on.

And forget about him for good.

CHAPTER THREE
Circus

My house is an architectural marvel. At least that's what the magazines it's been featured in say.

All high ceilings and carved beams and a giant wall of glass that overlooks the creek in the gulley with the golden cliff faces of Crown Trails to the right.

I've filled it with expensive furniture and a photography studio, and every room has a range of plants from cacti to spider plants to string of pearls ... But it still feels *so* fucking lifeless.

When Mom and Dad died, I'd gotten a big chunk of insurance money and an even bigger inheritance. The first thing I'd done was sell the house we lived in, clear some land in the middle of the forest, and build the biggest house I could fit. This is going to be my forever home. The place where I start a family with a thousand kids, and while I might be young, I'm ready for that to happen.

Mentally.

Emotionally, I'm still struggling.

And physically, the house is still an empty shell.

I watch the sunrise from my living room like I do

every morning. The sky is already a pale orange and the cliff faces look on fire. It never fails to make me fall in love with the world again, even if the world has forgotten about me.

My post last night at least seems to have gained some traction. I'm lying on a black chaise with matching print shirt and shorts I was sent from one of my favorite eco-friendly designers. The color pops and I've got my angles right.

Even I'm happy with the way that one turned out.

Still, I could be doing more. My interactions could be higher. I take a photo of the sunrise and caption it "good morning" before adding it to my story, and I smile as all the good mornings and good nights start to come through.

I love my followers, and I love the brands I'm starting to build working relationships with.

But I need more.

More followers, more endorsements, more modeling contracts, and maybe, one day, some acting roles.

A movie.

That's the end goal.

Because if I'm internationally known, I'll never be lonely again.

Baby steps, I remind myself.

Time to get on with my plan.

Leon has the day off and is going to start the demo on the back end of his house, so I get dressed in worn jeans and a floral tank top before biking over to meet him.

Will I actually help with the house? Unlikely.

But Leon is my last hope for this stupid swimwear thing.

Royce would have been perfect if not for his complete hatred of attention, and Tanner has the right body shape I'm going for but has nothing to make him stand out. Laura and Rafe seem to have withdrawn lately, and I can only hope they're working on their issues, and Dahlia said doing it wouldn't be a great image for a schoolteacher.

I'd ask Jules, but she and Mitch are pretty conservative, and wearing something like a bathing suit would probably be too much for her.

Leon ... is far from what I was imagining. I've been lurking a few influencers over the past few days, and they're mostly traditionally hot. Sculpted, slim bodies, nice tan, minimal hair.

I love Leon to hell, but he's the complete opposite of that. Thick, hairy, and rough are three words I'd use to describe him, and his arms and body are a variety of different skin tones from working in the sun so much.

Still, I have a day left to get back to *Royals*, so I need to get this done.

"Morning," he grunts as he opens his front door.

"It's okay, the cavalry has arrived."

He pretends to glance behind me. "Please tell me

you're referring to a horde of invisible badasses because you can't be talking about you."

I nudge him and walk through to his kitchen. It's half torn apart, but there's still enough countertop for me to jump up and sit on. "I've come to lend my services."

"Oh, you have? Why don't you start by tearing down that awning over there?"

I glance at the offending overhang. "My *conversational* services. You know work always goes faster when you have a friend around."

"Maybe when that friend's not you." His eyes crinkle at the corners as he crosses his arms. "I'm not doing it."

"Sorry, what?"

"The photo thing. You know I don't have time. I get one day a week off, and this place is at least a month behind schedule."

"It would just be *one* day."

"Sorry, Circus, not happening."

I slump. "Who told you, anyway?"

"Tanner gave me the heads-up."

"Of course he did." I resist rolling my eyes and jump down from the counter. Even if he won't help me—and I know him well enough to know pushing won't work—I'm still planning to help out here.

We spend the better part of the day with Leon tearing shit off the back of his house and me carting the debris to a massive dumpster.

"I really am sorry I can't help out," he finally says

when we stop for some water.

"I know you are."

"It's just this contract I have coming up, and then there's still a ton of smaller jobs I've booked."

I smirk at his overapologizing, because I know Leon means it. "It's totally cool, I get it. Maybe I just need to call them and say I can't do it."

"Would that be a bad thing?"

Terrible, actually, but I can't tell Leon that. We're as close as brothers, but I'm self-aware enough to know that using all those notifications as a form of validation probably isn't healthy, and I'm too embarrassed to explain that to someone as emotionally stable as Leon. "It wouldn't be the best thing when it comes to getting more brands on board. I dunno ... maybe I can still find someone else ..."

His head turns sharply. "You're not taking Rowan Harvey up on his offer."

"Whoa, how much did Tanner tell you?"

"Everything. People want to know what happened between you two." He chuckles. "It's obvious enough that even Tanner picked up on it."

"And what did you tell him?" I should know better than to ask though. Leon's known the whole time and kept it to himself.

"What do you think? It's not *for* me to tell. That's up to you. But I'm still pissed you didn't report him for assault."

What was the point? He was gone from Sunbury before I could even talk to him about it. He ignored my calls and messages, and two days later, his number was disconnected.

I know reporting it would probably have been the smart choice, and five years later I feel like an idiot for having been too blinded by my crush on him to make it.

"Yeah, I know you are. Even considering his offer is stupid."

"Then why are you?"

"Can you get out of my head?" I push him playfully, but he doesn't budge.

"Circus ..."

"Look, it's fine. I'm not considering, whatever. Don't stress."

He sighs because obviously he doesn't believe *that* statement, and I mean, I can't imagine why. I really went for convincing.

It's a little hard to be convincing when *you* don't even believe the shit coming out of your mouth.

The problem is, I do feel like adding more of that sex factor will boost my audience and have more people wanting to work with me. Good pictures lead to actual contracts like the one I did for a body spray last year. And contracts lead to more exposure, and more exposure leads to the kind of die-hard fans who are just waiting to message me good morning.

The thing is, I don't want fame. Not exactly.

I want the love and attention that comes with it.

And as much as I've been trying to push it from my mind, Rowan would look *so* hot in those swimsuits. Even through his shirts, I can tell he has a great body, and his tattoos will pop. They're that "interest factor" I'm after.

It just sucks that the body and tats are attached to *him.*

I'm still no closer to making a decision when I head back home again. I'm gritty and my hair is gross, so I snap a quick shot to add to my story as evidence of me doing *real* work, then jump in the shower and wash it all away.

My screen is full of notifications by the time I jump out, and it warms my heart.

I head to my bedroom to change, but I'm still so absorbed by my thoughts that I flop back on my bed just wearing my towel. It's times like this that I try to imagine the advice Mom and Dad would have given me. But I swear with every anniversary, their voices are getting quieter.

I take a deep breath and close my eyes, picturing Mom's face. I imagine telling her what really happened on prom night, and instantly her kind eyes turn savage and I can see her jumping straight on the phone to Mrs. Harvey to curse her to hell. I can see Dad's sympathy and feel his support as he squeezes my shoulder.

I know exactly what they'd both say.

Mom would tell me to use his offer as an

opportunity for revenge.

Dad would tell me to think logically and remember I'm running a business.

Both of their suggestions are tempting too. I'd love to get revenge after all these years, but I'm too much like Dad to follow through on it. That said, Mom's savage streaks hit me rarely, but when they do, I can be vicious.

I glance at the Magic 8-Ball sitting on my side table.

It's how I make choices when I'm completely torn over which way to go.

And so far, it hasn't steered me wrong.

With a deep breath, I push up and grab it, then give it a good shake.

"Should I let Rowan do this shoot with me?"

I hold my breath as the option bobs to the top.

As I see it, yes.

CHAPTER FOUR
ROWAN

Wow.

I stare at the photo Circus just posted for a moment, until I come to my senses and quickly stash the phone in my pocket. My grandma would hit the roof if she caught me drooling over a picture of a guy, and my grandpa ... he might be getting old, but I don't want to think about what he would do.

I duck down to check the casserole Grandma put in the oven as she slices a salad to go with it. Late last year, Mom and Dad decided that moving Mom's parents into a little cottage out back would be good for the whole family. It means less stress on my parents while they work at the diner all day, and someone to keep an eye on my grandparents as they get older.

Mom and Dad have always had a strong sense of family responsibility.

Too bad I wasn't factored into this decision.

The house already feels too small for me and my parents, but adding my grandparents to the mix makes it downright claustrophobic. I can't even let myself *think* about the picture of Circus, covered in dirt, clearly about to shower, without being convinced my grandpa can hear my thoughts.

So I clench my jaw and ignore them.

Just like I've always done.

Still, it was no better when I was in Portland either. I only slipped a couple of times, and went to a gay club to pick up, but all I could worry about was if I'd get caught. Ninety miles wasn't enough distance.

"What do you have cooking in here?" Grandpa asks, walking into the kitchen for another ginger ale.

"We're doing a casserole."

"Ah, helping, are you?" His expression darkens. "That city's turned you soft. Why don't you come watch the football game with me?"

"Thanks, but we're almost done."

He *hmphs*. "I'm sure your gran has got it sorted."

"Then I guess I'll take a shower."

"Suit yourself." He sneers a little as he heads back through to the living room.

Well, I'm not going to subject myself to him calling the players names that he somehow still thinks are okay to use. No, thank you.

Instead, I climb the stairs to my room and close the door firmly behind myself.

The lack of privacy is just one of the annoyances grating at me, and every time I picture Circus and his *fucking twenty-five grand* it makes my blood hot. The things I could do with that kind of money.

I wouldn't be living in this house, for a start. I could actually look at putting my Sports Science degree to good use.

I almost, for the hundredth time this week, go to call Tanner, whose number I stole off my sister, just to try and get in touch with Circus.

He holds all the cards.

And I'm sure he had no problem with getting someone else to help out, but I won't deny the thought of taking sexy shots with him is appealing too.

I *shouldn't* find it appealing, and I wish I could be stronger when it comes to thinking about him, but he's so attractive it isn't fair.

I'm trying to work out how to come to terms with being gay, while finding balance with the man my family expects me to be. But then I think of that photo, and my dick gets interested, and I open a game on my phone instead. Every time I consider jerking off, I distract my hands with whatever the closest mindless task is, and because of that habit, I've become pretty good at these stupid racing games.

Definitely not a life achievement I'm proud of.

Five minutes later and my problem still hasn't gone away. My dick digs into the mattress, and I swear I've never been as horny as I have been in the weeks since I returned to Sunbury.

Then again, high school was pretty fucking rough. All those lunchtimes I'd sit opposite Circus and watch his lips. All those weekends we'd hike Crown Trails and Circus's hand would brush mine. All those Sunday mornings we'd sit in church and catch each other's eyes, and I'd try, like the good Catholic boy I was, to pay attention to the sermon and not on what Circus's skin would taste like.

There's a knock on the front door, then quiet voices downstairs before my gran calls up for me.

I have no clue who it could be, because most of my friends from high school moved on from Sunbury, and the one or two who stuck around aren't people I've wanted to stay in contact with.

I walk downstairs and almost trip over my feet when I see Circus waiting on the front porch. *Okay, Rowan, be cool.*

I ignore my rapid heartbeat and lean against the doorframe. He hasn't noticed me yet, so I give myself a moment to study him up close. The long chain earring and black septum piercing I've studied in countless photos. His perfect, clear skin, his long dark eyebrows. That shaggy hair.

That immediately pull together when he catches sight of me.

"Hey." That one word sounds painful to get out. And not just because of his scratchy voice, but the heavy tone it carries.

"Afternoon." I try to match his mood. If he wants to be shitty with me, then fine. It's justified, after all. And when he can barely stand the sight of me, it sure makes resisting him easier to handle.

"You got a second?"

"Sure." I don't make a move to invite him in. That would be way too close for comfort.

"I want to talk to you about this job."

I can't help it—I smile. And then quickly remember I'm not supposed to be doing that. "What about it?"

"I can't do it solo."

"So I heard."

"*So* I accept your offer."

I glance over my shoulder to check no one is listening in, but I can't be sure. Stepping outside, I pull the door closed behind me. "I'm in."

"Just like that, huh?"

"Not exactly." I think about the implications of this job. Mostly naked pictures of me and another man. Not an easy thing to explain away to your homophobic family. "I have …" How can I leverage this without pushing too hard? "Two conditions."

"Of course you do. Let's hear them."

"First, the pictures can't have my face in them. No tagging, nothing that can be immediately linked back to me."

"Yeah, right." He starts to laugh. "What about your tattoos?"

"Plenty of guys have sleeves, and none of my work is anything specific. If someone recognizes me based on those, good on them. But no face. No tagging. I mean it."

Circus steps back and leans against the railing. He doesn't answer immediately, and for a moment I'm worried I pushed too far. If he wants my face in these shots, then fine, for twenty-five K I'll do it, but the backlash if any of my family sees them will mean taking my money and running.

But ... maybe it's time to do that anyway. I can't live the kind of life I want to here. I'm too on edge, too worried about doing the wrong thing.

If I do this job and move back to Portland, maybe then I can go back to my psychologist. Let myself feel these emotions I've always been told are wrong. Because I've never felt more alive than in the back halls of the school, with Circus's mouth on mine.

"Fine," he finally says. "I can make it work without our faces. Or yours, at least."

Relief weighs down my limbs. And if I thought I'd been pushing my luck with that first request, this next one is really going to test how badly he needs me. "One more thing."

"Seriously? The money and me rearranging my plans for the photos isn't enough?"

I can't look at him. "This won't require any work on your behalf."

"Why don't I believe you?"

I almost go to call him Kelly but hold back. "When I was in Portland, I tried to move on with my life. I met a nice girl, we leased an apartment off campus, but no matter how much I just wanted to put this place behind me, I couldn't. Because I can't shake how guilty I feel over what I did to you."

Circus shrugs. "I'm missing how this is my problem."

"I want to move on. I'm tired."

"I'm cool with it. Trust me, holding a grudge takes a whole lot less energy than you'd think."

I'm frustrated, but I keep my cool. "Look, you can keep the money if you have to." It kills me to say that. "This is what I need. Some closure. Once I have that—"

"You'll leave."

"What?"

"You do this job, you get your money, your *forgiveness*." His voice is mocking. "Then you leave. For *good* this time."

My mouth drops. This isn't the detached coolness he's been giving me lately, there's actual hatred burning behind his words. It makes me feel sick. It makes me hate myself as I go back and replay that moment over and over in my mind. Not for the first time, I wish I could take it back.

Where the hell would I be now if I could?

His terms should be easy to agree to. It's what I'd literally just been considering, but as much as this small town can feel stifling at times, it's home. Given the chance to leave, for good, I'm not totally convinced I'd take it.

But I'm not going to tell Circus that.

And if what he needs to forgive me is for me to leave, then fine.

"Okay, deal."

I'm expecting him to hold out his hand or something, but he stays firmly planted on the other side of the porch

"To be clear, when we're shooting, you'll follow all directions I give you. We don't have to like each other, we don't have to talk, we don't even have to be civil, but we do need to take hot photos. So you'll shut up, you'll listen, and you'll do what I say. Then when it's over, we never have to speak to each other again."

"Sounds good."

He laughs. "It sounds like fucking magic."

"Your eagerness to get rid of me does wonders for my ego." If I thought joking would help lighten a little of the tension between us, I'm dead wrong.

"Oh yeah? Try giving head for the first time and getting your nose broken for your efforts. Then you can tell me how your ego's going."

What the hell?

He jogs down the front steps, grabs his bike, and takes off. I'm too busy reeling from his words that I forget I'm not supposed to be watching the way his ass moves as he pedals down the drive.

I broke his nose?

From one punch?

If I felt like shit before, it's nothing to the gross feelings creeping over me now. I try to remember the way his nose used to look and if it's any different now, but I'm struggling to remember.

And it's not like it matters.

At the end of the day, I fucked up, and now I'm paying for it.

As I should be.

Yet somehow, Circus is taking this chance on me anyway.

Which means I have to do everything in my power to make sure these are the sexiest shots he's ever seen in his life.

FAKE FRIENDS

CHAPTER FIVE
Circus

I'm up way too late the night before the shoot, setting everything up, so I sleep past sunrise the next morning. Never a good sign.

I figure we'll take a few different shots in my studio, then head down to get some by the creek.

At first, Rowan's need to keep his face out of the pictures stumped me, but I like a challenge. I'm sure I can make it work.

The thing I'm unsure about is if either of us will be able to act natural around each other. There's so much tension between us that even trying to have a relatively easy conversation the other day ended with me needing to put some distance between us. And we'll be here. All alone.

With one tiny scrap of material between us.

Except none of that matters because I have a little thing called self-control.

Probably.

Rowan is getting here just after his shift ends at midday, which means I have a whole morning to fill. I take a short hike along Crown Trails, then come home and do some light exercises in my gym. I make a fruit smoothie and cook lunch and spend time walking around watering every plant I own.

Normally I'm okay with just being still.

But every minute feels weighted with purpose and pressures me to keep moving.

I have no idea what he'll think of my place. The houses in Sunbury are small, idealistic homes where families come together, just like the Harvey's. It's an ice-blue cottage with a white front porch and window shutters. Is that the kind of thing Rowan likes?

Does it *matter* if he likes my place?

I tell myself it only matters because other than Leon, who helped out during the build, no one has been here. It's my space, and I like that it's hidden from the rest of the town.

With any luck, Rowan won't be able to find it, and all this stress will be for nothing.

I'm still torn about whether that would be the best-case scenario or not. Letting the brand down would be fucked-up for my career, but on the flip side, letting my guard down around Rowan could be fucked-up in other ways.

Because I really do hate him.

And the messed-up thing is that it's not even totally over breaking my nose. That hurt, physically *and* emotionally, but I know if he'd stayed in town and we'd talked it out, I would have forgiven him. Immediately.

That's why I kept trying to get in contact with him.

I *wanted* to forgive him. I know what his family's like, and how he's struggled with his sexuality—I'm not an idiot. And yeah, I was angry at what he did, but I knew we could have gotten past it. I wanted to. That's why I never told anyone.

I was so far in love with him I was prepared to let him assault me and get away with it.

And that shit right there is *not* cool.

Which is why I told him he had to leave again.

I've always been weak when it comes to Rowan Harvey, and I refuse to give in again.

But isn't that what you're doing?

I tell the voice to fuck off.

Tires crunching the gravel on the outside of my house immediately set me on edge.

I guess he didn't miss the turnoff, then.

And like that, I have no idea how to act.

Do I meet him out front or give him time to ring the doorbell and make him wait?

What am I saying? *I* can't wait. This morning has been bad enough.

The whole way to the front door, I draw up my anger. I remind myself of how he left and how he broke my heart.

How he turned his back and I didn't cross his mind again.

I throw the front door open and watch as Rowan

gets out of his car. His mouth has hit the ground, and I pretend like I'm not studying him as he walks down the entrance.

"This is ..."

"A house. Correct. Come inside." The fewer words, the better.

"This is not a house. Where I live is a house. This is a stinking mansion."

"Don't be so dramatic." I step away from the doorway to let him past and push the door closed with a soft click.

The house is silent.

Rowan's eyes are huge as he looks around the entry hall, and I try to see what he sees. Glass panels on either side of the door extend all the way up to the ten-foot ceiling, revealing the bamboo outside. The beamed ceiling is painted black, the floors are polished cement, and above the shoe stand is a painting that takes up the entire wall.

Okay, I might have gone a little overboard.

"Let me show you around." I keep my tone dry, hiding the way his awe is sparking a little pride in my chest.

The far side of the house has the bedrooms, the middle is my studio, and on the right are the living areas.

"This is insane," Rowan finally says. "How the hell doesn't anyone know this is here?"

"Because I don't run my mouth, and you won't

either."

"You're seriously telling me no one has stumbled on this place?"

I move to the fridge to get us both a water. "Never. The only people who come out this way are looking to go hiking, and the massive *Keep Out* sign on my drive deters people from taking the wrong turn."

"You don't get scared out here on your own?"

Not the way he's thinking. Am I scared of someone lurking in the woods? Nope. Am I scared that the house will only ever be a lonely shell? Definitely. "No. You need to shower?"

"Unless you want me smelling like fries all day."

There are so many quips I could throw back. So many flirty one-liners I would have spouted back in the day, when I was trying to break his resolve.

"Back down that hall to the right."

He goes to step past me when I catch his shoulder. "Wait. Take off your shirt."

"Umm, now?"

"Yes."

He's clearly confused, but he reaches down and peels off his T-shirt.

My hunch was correct.

Smooth muscle, tanned skin, minor blemishes that I like too much to touch up. The curve of his sculpted back ... I shake my head. Umm, photos. It'll all look perfect for the photos.

"Now your shorts."

"What?"

"I need to know if there's any manscaping to do."

His confident smile takes over. "You volunteering?"

I keep my face blank. "The chance to cause you any kind of pain is definitely something I want in on."

He shoves his shorts down in one go, revealing black boxer briefs that are stretched over the curve of his ass.

I clear my throat, ignoring how well Rowan's filled out. And the tattoos ... definite weakness for me.

"Yeah, you're good." Did I check? Not well. But he's not overly hairy, and what he does have will look good.

I firmly turn my back as he walks away, determined not to let myself stare at his ass.

This is all business. Dad would have been proud of me for setting aside my personal thoughts and doing what's right for me.

Speaking of ...

I lift my phone, mess up my hair a little, then pull a cute face. I make sure to get Rowan's clothes, and a glimpse of his retreating form in the frame behind me.

Wanna know what I'm up to today?

As per our agreement there's no face, and he's too far away to make out much of anything. I upload the pic and head to the studio to start getting ready.

The range of swimwear goes from a tight G-string bottom to fun patterned board shorts. I already know it's going to take multiple reminders today that this is all strictly professional, because seeing his ass on full display is going to be the biggest test I've ever put myself through.

Right, then.

I've created the set to look like a beachside villa. Pull-down screen, blue-and-white striped sun lounges, and sand dusting the ground.

I grab a potted palm and add it, then fold a couple of towels as props in the corner. With the bright lights overhead, I'm satisfied it passes for outdoors.

I glance back at the swimsuits. Might as well get the hardest part out of the way first.

I grab one of the G-strings, kick out of my shorts, and quickly pull it on.

The shower cuts off somewhere down the hall, and a flood of butterflies let loose in my gut. I squish them down. This is my home, my domain, and no one is going to make me feel uncomfortable here.

I'm in charge.

My dick twitches, reminding me that's not the case at all.

It's going to be a long day.

FAKE FRIENDS

CHAPTER SIX
ROWAN

Walking in and seeing Circus with his ass out is literally the last thing a sexually frustrated gay man needs.

"What the hell is that?"

Circus glances down at what I'm assuming is a swimsuit and shrugs. "What we're wearing."

"*We* as in *both* of us?"

He picks up another one and tosses it my way.

Well, I guess this is happening.

I slide the tiniest bathing suit known to man on under my towel before pulling the towel from my hips and running it over my still-damp air.

"Sit." Circus points to a chair next to where he's clearly set up for us to shoot. And damn, he's got his grumpy pants on today. Looks like I don't need to worry about keeping my distance when he's doing it enough for us both.

"Are you planning on treating me like a dog all day?"

He just stares at me.

I'm not sure why his total lack of wanting to be around me makes me smile, but I somehow manage to resist as I do as I'm told. He steps close enough I can see goose bumps pebbling his skin, and then he turns on a hairdryer and sets to work.

I'll give it to him, he knows what he's doing.

He parts my dark blond hair to the side and makes it look all full and messy in a purposeful way, rather than the shag ball it usually is.

I force all of my focus straight ahead instead of on the smooth plains of his stomach.

"You remember no face, right?"

"Clearly, otherwise I'd be doing your makeup too."

"Ah, right." I clear my throat as he puts the hairdryer away and realize that it's time to do this.

"Okay. First few shots will be easy. Just lie on that sun lounger like you would if you were at the beach—"

"Wearing nothing—"

"And *relax*. The more into it you are, the better. If you're feeling awkward it'll definitely show, so just … don't do that. This might be some easy payday for you, but it's important to me, so I need you to take it seriously."

I salute. "Got it, Captain."

He doesn't find me amusing.

Circus takes his sun lounger and spreads out on his front. Completely without permission, my gaze tracks down his smooth back, to his sinfully round ass. It's a shade or two lighter than the rest of him, and I unconsciously lick my lips as my dick starts to take an interest.

Not the fuck now.

I quickly cross to my lounger and drop down onto my front, squashing my semi beneath me. A smarter man than me probably would have jerked off before coming here.

"Okay, just one photo like this, and then you should be on your back."

"What happened to not showing my face?"

"You'll put your arm over it, obviously. Then I'll edit the rest. Just a warning, most of the pictures I take are going to have your face." He smirks. "You're just going to have to trust me."

I don't like the sound of that. *Any* photos with my face involved could easily be "leaked" and wind up in my family's hands. "Umm ... you get why I don't want my face seen, right?"

He scoffs. "You gave me a broken nose, not amnesia. Of course I know, just like *you* should know I'm not a piece of shit who'll out you."

"I'm just saying—"

He sits up suddenly, eyes flashing. "*Stop* just saying. We're not here to chat. We're not catching up. We're doing a job. Now can you shut up and just do it?"

"No."

"*No?*"

I sit up and mirror him, waiting for him to meet my eyes. When he finally does, I remember how dangerous his stare can be. "I'm sorry."

Surprise flashes across his face.

"I know that doesn't make up for anything, but I am. What I did was wrong, and I've spent the last five years regretting it."

I can tell his guard is starting to slip, so I keep talking.

"I'm not saying we have to be friends, but can we at least try to drop this tension? If you want this to be natural, you're going to have to meet me halfway."

He's not sold. I get it. I've spent the last five years beating myself up over the dumbest thing I've ever done, so nothing Circus can say will top what I've already told myself.

I know exactly what he's thinking.

"Look, I'm an asshole. Can we just spend today acting like I'm not?"

"Fine." His long, full lips curl up at the sides. "Move over."

"What do you ..."

Oh, *oh*. Okay.

He shoves me across to the other side of my lounger and slides in beside me.

My brain short-circuits. His warm body presses against mine as he steers me facedown again. And there's, like, nothing between us.

My mouth is dry as he runs a hand down my back, and I have to remind myself this is all part of the photos.

"So, need me to do anything, or ..."

"Just lie there and be my prop." His normally gravelly voice is even scratchier than usual.

But like hell am I going to argue, because for some reason being his prop sounds really fucking hot.

I have no idea what exactly he's doing, but every time his leg slides over mine, or his chest touches my back, I have to hold in a groan.

I'm barely keeping it together when he nips my earlobe and gives my ass a solid squeeze.

"Shit." I jolt under his touch, but pulling back so I can see his face doesn't help solve my problem.

He's watching me steadily, clearly challenging me to leave.

Yeah, I'm not gonna do that.

With all my usual warning sensors in overdrive, I loop an arm around his waist and drag him closer. "You wanted sexy."

I pull Circus's leg over my hip and bury my face in his neck. Because how else am I supposed to hide my face?

And dear God. He feels incredible. All warm tight muscles and sharp jawline. I can't ever remember letting myself get this close to a man, and it's probably a good thing, because I can already tell how easy it would be to become addicted. To let go.

And I've been so good.

In my whole life I've only slipped a handful of times, but *damn* Circus makes me want to slip. To take everything that could have been mine and more.

Somehow, I behave.

Even when we get changed into proper swimsuits and he lays me back down, I manage to keep my hands to myself.

There's very little talking, and I can't tell if that's making the situation better or worse.

Circus slides across my body, resting his head on my chest, and I glance down under the hat resting over my face and watch his eyes fall closed.

He looks so peaceful.

So gorgeous.

I run my hand over his back, and suddenly, I really need this to end.

"Okay, that's enough pictures of us dry humping."

He slowly sits back up as I toss the hat aside. "Why? You're clearly enjoying it." Then he very obviously glances at the erection straining against my swimsuit.

I know what he's trying to do. He's trying to make me uncomfortable. And I am. More than I should be. Because as much as I want to embrace who I am, that voice in my head, telling me I'm wrong, is getting loud.

Even though it's making me feel sick, I ignore it and tuck my hands behind my head instead. "I thought we worked out years ago that this was my standard reaction to you."

"Yeah, well, a lot has changed since then."

"Are you dating anyone?"

"We're working."

"I'll take that as a no." I grin. "In which case, what's a few boners amongst colleagues?"

"Inappropriate?"

"Eh. If you didn't want it to happen, you wouldn't have grinded up all over me. I'm repressed as fuck, what did you expect?"

Circus gives me a weird look, then gets up and throws a pair of board shorts my way. We both change, with my dying to take a peek, and then he grabs some camera equipment and gestures for me to follow.

I still can't get over how enormous his house is. If I could dream up a mansion in the woods ... well, okay, it wouldn't have been *this* because I don't have the imagination, but wow.

"I can't believe you have this place all to yourself and I'm back in my childhood bedroom."

"Yeah, it must suck to be surrounded by your family."

I cringe at his words, wishing I could take everything back. While my biggest regret sits solidly with what I did to him, a very close second is not being there for him when his parents died. I know how close they all were because Mr. and Mrs. Atkins were gold-star parents.

I'm sure they knew about me. I'm sure they knew how I felt about Circus.

And I'd even put money down that when they saw his face and realized I'd ditched town, they would have known exactly what happened there too.

It makes me feel sick.

I want to give him a hug.

I don't, but I want to.

"When did you build this place?"

"After I lost my parents in that crash."

"What was the inspiration?"

He sets off across the lawn. "Big."

"Wow, that's deep."

His lips twitch. "Come on, down here."

I follow him down the gentle slope and through a thin line of trees to a creek. "What are we doing?"

"These photos are going to be more candid, natural ones. Just get in the water and do whatever. Try and keep your back to the camera where you can."

Shouldn't be a problem. Circus sets up the camera on a tripod, then takes some time to adjust settings or whatever he's working on. None of it makes any sense to me.

I just look around and try to take in nature.

It's not often I'm surrounded by this much quiet. Sunbury is a sleepy kinda town, but my house decidedly is not. Out here, I can hear myself think.

I guess I understand why Circus built his place out here.

The soft lap of waves against skin lets me know Circus has waded into the water behind me. I glance at him over my shoulder, trying to calm my racing heart.

His board shorts barely cover his ass, and they're in a bright tropical print, like most of the clothes he seems to wear these days.

When he gets close enough, I reach out and tug the chain dangling from his ear. "I like this."

"Oh yeah?"

He turns his head to look across the creek and smiles wide. It takes me a moment to realize he's posing for a shot, and I hurry to do the same. Then I decide to have fun with it.

I send a gush of water his way, then quickly dart back as he retaliates. He holds up a hand. "This is fine, but hair and makeup, remember?"

"Nothing above the shoulders." I wink. "Got it."

And even if it's all for some photos, Circus lets himself have fun. His smile, the way his eyes light up, the way the sun slipping between the leaves plays over his skin, all make it impossible to look away.

I use every opportunity I can to get my hands on him.

And I give myself free rein to enjoy this for the day.

As he takes up a pose, holding on to my arm, I catch him around the waist and throw him over my shoulder instead. His skin smells like water and sunshine, and I wonder again what he tastes like.

It's lucky we're only doing this once because I'm quickly becoming as addicted to him as I used to be.

And I can't let that happen.

I slowly set Circus down, loving the feel of his torso brushing mine, but even when his feet are on the creek bed, I can't let him go.

My gaze settles on his nose, where I notice a bump about halfway. There's my proof, then. The permanent reminder of what I did slices through my heart.

I lean down and press my lips to it.

Circus's eyes fall closed for a moment, and I allow myself the briefest hope that maybe we can be okay. Maybe I can make up for what I did and we can move on.

I have no idea what I want us to move on *to* when I know I can't stay in Sunbury long term. Not unless I either want to be disowned or settle down with a woman. And I've already discovered I can't go through with that ploy.

Circus jerks back out of my arms. "I think we're done."

"Really? That's ... it?" Why am I disappointed when I should be relieved?

"Yep. I can do the editing stuff solo. Thanks for your help."

He's already out of the water and pulling down the tripod by the time I reach him.

"You okay?"

"Perfect. I have my pictures, and as soon as the money is in my account, I'll send over your share."

"But ..."

"But what? I pretended like you aren't an asshole for

a day, and now I accept your apology. You can move on." He throws the tripod over his shoulder as he starts to walk away. "And remember to do that far away from Sunbury."

FAKE FRIENDS

CHAPTER SEVEN
CIRCUS

This. Is. Bad.

I flick through photo after photo of perfection.

And I hate to say it, but Rowan makes me look good. The tats, the unruly hair, the confidence in how he holds himself.

He's come a long way since high school.

Back then he was guarded and scared, and the only place he looked like he owned his skin was on the football field. Still, he always caught my eye. Always drew out that curious side of me that was attracted to what I didn't know.

The first time I went to his house after school, I remember overhearing his dad asking who the little pretty boy was. And I knew by his tone what he was really asking.

First: Is that kid gay?

Second: What the fuck is he doing with my son?

I was never a favorite around his place, especially when his grandparents were there, so we spent as much time at my house, or wandering Crown Trails, as we could.

And as I pause over the photo of Rowan kissing my nose, an irrational surge of anger passes through me.

I was there, for years, in the secret, stolen moments of his life. I was the only one who knew his secret, and the only one who didn't push for him to figure himself out.

All I did was wait.

Show him it was okay.

And that night, when he finally kissed me and we gave in to a year of sexual tension, I kissed him like we meant forever.

I had no idea forever would last all of five minutes.

It would be so easy to fall into the rabbit hole of wondering what life would have been like if he'd never left, but I refuse to let myself.

I refuse to think about anything but the fact he's about to leave again, and then life can go back to how it used to be.

He's still closeted, and I doubt that will ever change.

Way too much drama for me.

Instead, I'll take my plants and my little piece of the internet and just keep doing what I love.

I search the couch for my phone, suddenly realizing I haven't checked my notifications all day.

Rookie error, and reason number ninety-seven for why I need to keep Rowan at arm's length.

I open the app and scramble to sit upright.

Is this legit?

People are going batshit over the photo I snapped earlier.

And they all want to know one thing.

Who's the guy?

I've made it no secret that I'm pansexual, but I've never shared anything before that had someone else in it, not even friends.

And apparently, that was a good move on my behalf.

The more comments and replies I scroll through, the happier my mood gets. It feels like plugging in and recharging my battery, and even as I read through responses from hours ago, more are coming in.

I open my emails and find one already waiting from my manager. Of course he's seen the photo and is next-level excited about it. And of *course* they want the *Royal Swimwear* shots, stat. I reply and let him know I'll have some ready by morning.

Almost immediately, my phone starts to ring.

"You need to post one now," he says, without so much as a hello.

"None of them are edited."

"So post a candid, I don't care. Terri from *Royals* wants his brand on your page ASAP."

What I can't tell him is that mostly all of the candid shots have Rowan's face in them. It's going to take some editing to make cropping him out of them look any good. But it's not like I can say no.

"Give me an hour."

"Good stuff, Circus. And whoever that guy is, good pick."

"Thanks."

We hang up and I stare at my phone, wondering if this is what whiplash feels like.

Not that I have long to ponder that because, with only fifty-nine minutes to go, I have my work cut out for me.

Most of the shots in the studio have Rowan's face artfully hidden, but they'll be the ones the brand wants to use. They're more professional and polished. The ones by the creek are mostly for me. I try to have my page looking as unstaged as possible, which means playing with these shots until we look like we're just out having spontaneous fun.

From one photo to the next, it really is starting to bug me how good Rowan is at this. And how annoyed I am that we have to hide his face. Because that smile ... it used to be the rarest thing about him and never failed to make my knees weak.

Nope.

Next.

I eventually find a shot with Rowan's back to the camera. It must have been one of the earlier ones we took. But his ass is showcasing those trunks, and the way he's dragging his hand back through his hair has his back muscles on point.

My forehead's resting on his relaxed shoulder as I

look down into the water, and while this shot isn't the fun, vibrant look I was going for, there's something else here.

Something more intimate.

It reminds me of a quiet moment during stolen time and sums up exactly how our relationship used to be.

Plus, the swimwear looks great.

Which is *obviously* the most important thing here.

I do some light editing to make sure everything looks sharp, then increase the green light being diffused by the trees. It looks ethereal and cool. I almost don't want to share it.

But I do, because this is work.

I write the caption, *Outdoors with him*.

People can make whatever they want of that. I add a quick line about the brand and then upload it.

The picture has barely been live for a second when it starts.

And while I love the interaction and the flood of attention and all my happy chemicals are buzzing, it's all a bit much right now.

Because it comes with a tinge of sadness.

They don't love me. They love me *and* Rowan, and that's not a concept that exists. It's not even one I can milk for attention because as soon as this payment clears, he'll be out of my life for good.

***

"Circus fucking Atkins!"

Oops. The loud voice booming from my front hall makes me scramble to duck down behind my couch and hope Leon gets bored and goes home.

No such luck.

"I know you're here! Your bike and car are both out front."

He doesn't know I didn't go for a hike.

"I'm not leaving until you come out."

Urg. Persistent bastard.

I poke my head out from behind the couch and find him already looking at me. I grin. "Knew I was there, huh?"

"The whole time."

I clear my throat and sit back on the couch, trying to act natural. "So, what brings you here?"

"Cut the shit, Circus. Tell me that wasn't Rowan Harvey in that photo."

"Photo …" I tap my chin.

He pins me with a look.

"Naw, you're not as scary as you think you are."

He sighs and drops onto the couch beside me. "I'm worried."

"It was just a few photos. I needed this job, and he needed the money. It was a win-win."

"Why did you need the job?"

"Because I have to expand my reach."

"But *why*? You already have a ton of followers and get sent a heap of shit, and it's not like you need the money."

"You're theorizing, aren't you?"

"Might be."

I laugh. "Okay, and what are you reading into this situation?"

He slants a quick look my way then crosses his arms. "I'm worried you're doing this as an excuse to spend time with him."

"One whole day where we hardly spoke. Total master plan."

"Be serious. Tell me you're completely over him and I'll let it drop."

"I'm so over him that the deal for these photos is that he leaves Sunbury again. Happy?"

Leon's eyebrows shoot up. "Wasn't expecting that."

"See? I'm capable of making actual life decisions."

"Jury's still out on that."

"You'll see." I throw a cushion at him. "Wanna stay for dinner?"

"Sorry, man, can't. I've got a *date*." He widens his eyes like this is a totally new concept, but even with his busy schedule I swear he has a new date each week.

"Well, good luck with this one."

He hums. "I don't have good vibes."

"Then why go?"

"Because we're not all celibate hermits, like you."

I raise my eyes to the ceiling. "Celibate, my ass."

"Exactly my point."

"We can't all be whores like you. I get enough."

"Oh, yeah? When was the last time you picked up?"

"It's been, like …" A month? Two?

Leon pats my shoulder as he stands up. "You keep saying you want a big family, but I don't see you out there making it happen. Forget about Rowan. You deserve better."

I snort because I'm mature like that. "He's already forgotten."

I walk Leon to the front door and close it behind him. The click echoes loudly through the entrance, and the silence that follows presses down on me.

Because there's still so much night left ahead, I stand there and wait until he drives away, reminding myself that I really am alone.

Leon on his date.

Royce and Tanner all loved up.

Rafe not answering his phone.

Dahlia working on tomorrow's course work, and Jules and Mitch running tonight's youth group.

I drop my head against the solid front door and contemplate making dinner for one.

Then I head in the opposite direction and go to bed instead.

CHAPTER EIGHT
ROWAN

The first thing I see when I wake up is the photo Circus has posted of the two of us. I stare at it for longer than I should. At his round shoulders and all that smooth brown skin. It's a side-on shot of him, but even in profile I'm more drawn to him than I've ever been.

I clench my jaw and close out of the photo.

Now he's forgiven me and this job is done, there's nothing tying us together anymore. I can officially move on.

That thought should fill me with optimism; I have my forgiveness, will get a huge payday, and can leave Sunbury. Maybe I can even live the life I've always wanted for myself.

But while the whole idea of moving away seems appealing at first thought—freedom, anonymity, complete agency over my life—Sunbury has always been my home.

I thought that once I had my forgiveness I'd be done. I could run back to Portland and put all this behind me.

There's still something missing though.

So Circus asking me to leave and never come back ...

I don't know if I can.

I throw my phone on the bed and change into some running gear. There are no gyms in Sunbury which means staying fit, you know, until I *leave*, will take more effort than it used to. And I didn't work for years on building this muscle just so I can waste away now.

My grandma calls out to me when I reach the bottom of the stairs. "I've cooked breakfast, honey, come and eat."

And has she ever. Hash browns, bacon, eggs, sausage, and a buttload of sides. I swear sometimes she forgets she's not cooking for a whole diner anymore.

"Sorry." I kiss her on the head. "I'm just heading out. Save me some and I'll eat when I'm back."

"Okay, but it won't keep well," she warns me. "Where are you going?"

"For a run. I need to stay fit."

She gives me a sweet smile and pats me on the back. "Yes, you have to keep looking sharp. You need to find a nice girl soon. Thank goodness Leita gave me great-grandbabies, or I might never live to see the day."

Somehow I keep my smile in place. "Be back later."

I leave as fast as I can.

My jog takes me through the quiet residential streets of Sunbury, and I breathe in the clean morning air. It's a different vibe than Portland, for sure. Leaving my apartment in the city at this time would have meant weaving my way through people on their morning commute.

I enjoyed living there. It was a change of scene.

But if I'm honest, this is where I belong.

I run down to the fairground and lap the large oval a couple of times, before heading back into town. My muscles are burning, and my shirt is stuck to my back with sweat, like it normally is after a good workout. I love the feeling.

"Rowan, hey!"

Speak of the devil. My oldest sister is sitting at a table out the front of Peg's cafe with a few of her mom friends.

I smirk as I approach. "Supporting the competition? Wait until I tell our parents."

She flips me the bird while she rocks the stroller beside her back and forth. "They do better coffee here, and it's all organic."

I gasp like she's just told me she murdered someone last night. "You're an abomination."

Leita introduces me to her two friends while I duck my head under the stroller to see my nephew. His cheeks are bright, and he's gnawing on some rubber thing like he's determined to make it breakfast.

"He okay?" I ask.

"Teething."

I nod like that explains so much. "Where are the other two?"

"Daycare. Today's my free day."

Since we were younger, Leita's entire life goal was to become a mom and do all the Stepford Wives shit. Because of that, she refused point-blank to work at Harvey's which meant Piper and I had to pick up the slack.

She and Piper have never gotten along, but some days I wish I could be more like Leita. She doesn't care what anyone thinks of her.

"I'll come around this week and take my nephew out. Then you'll have an *actual* free day."

"Perfect! I'm in desperate need of a workout."

I laugh. "Why?"

"Because Laurie has worked all week, and the gym in Port Welling doesn't have a childcare."

I smile in pity, like I know all about it, and then glance over at the person coming out of the cafe.

As soon as he sees me, Circus pulls up short.

"Rowan." He tilts his head my way and keeps walking.

I watch his back, focused on the dolphin-print shirt, fighting every stupid reason my brain comes up with to go over there.

I don't want this to be it. I don't want one scratchy, barely polite version of my name to be the last thing he says to me.

"Gotta go." I duck down again to kiss my nephew on the foot, then jog after Circus, determined to catch him.

I've barely rounded the corner onto O'Connell Road,

when I stumble to a stop. He's *right there* leaning against the wall next to his bike, like he has all the time in the world.

"Ah, hey." *Not* what I wanted to say to him, but he makes my brain stupid.

"Following me?" There's the slightest teasing hint to his words that I'm not sure if I'm imagining.

"No, just ... out for a jog."

"Carry on, then." He waves his hand the way I was headed, calling my bluff.

I'm about a second away from just leaving, when I remind myself I'm not chickenshit. "Actually, I wanted to know how the shots turned out."

He narrows his eyes a little, and I know he doesn't believe me, though I can't imagine why when I literally pulled that from my ass. "Good."

That's all he's giving me? Sheesh, don't make it easy or anything. The conversation turns stale, and I know the smart thing to do would be to leave and put him behind me, but I don't want to. Because with him, I've never done the smart thing.

All those Sundays in church when I should have been paying attention, all those years of high school where I should have been focusing on studying and playing ball, instead I was too busy working out how we could be friends.

And all those days during senior year where I should have been hanging out with the people I'd been close to for years, instead of sneaking off with the guy I couldn't stop thinking about.

My issues ran a lot deeper then, but even now I'm struggling to accept who I am.

And if I'm still not ready to pursue something with a guy, I should keep running.

But Circus makes me want to be ready. He makes me want to beg him for another chance.

Even though I know he'll never give it to me.

So instead of being *smart*, I ask, "Can I come see them?"

He scowls. "I *told* you I'd take your face out, and I have."

"That's not what I ..." I shake my head. "I just want to see how they've turned out."

I watch as his eyes slowly drop from my face, down my sweaty shirt to my legs, and a shiver rips down my spine. I'm expecting him to say he'll send them to me or that I can wait until they're online. So I'm caught off guard when he agrees.

"Tonight. Bring dinner with you."

Then he grabs his bike, swings one leg over, and heads off down the street.

My hands are shaking.

I think of the implications of taking dinner to his house and being there alone while we look at photographic evidence of our day yesterday.

I'm getting ahead of myself.

Even if I was thrown into a porn-like situation with Circus, there's no way I'd follow through with it.

I'd bet Circus has had guys and girls after him his entire life, and with the pick of the bunch, why would he want some inexperienced loser like me?

After what I did, there's no way he could ever trust me again. I have no right to these thoughts about him, and I wish I had enough self-control to turn them off and move on.

I remind myself it's what I need to do.

My brain reminds my common sense to kindly fuck off.

I can't escape my nerves all day. It was like this at the burger house yesterday while I was working. At least then I had a constant stream of orders to keep me busy.

Dinner is a bigger thing than it should be too. Do I go buy something? Grab takeout? Jesus, I don't even know what he likes.

I bite the inside of my cheek as I grab my phone and hover over my sister's number. She's been working at the diner for years, so surely if anyone knows what people eat around here, it'd be her.

But ... that could also lead to questions I don't want to answer. And I have no idea how Piper would react if she found out I was gay. She's had the biggest crush on Tanner since school and then a few months back he shacked up with his male best friend.

It sort of puts a damper on things.

Maybe I can approach this a different way. Tanner has always been friendly, after all.

This phone call is going to be awkward, but no less awkward than asking Piper.

He answers straightaway.

"Hello?"

"Ah, hey, Tanner?"

"Speaking."

"This is Rowan Harvey."

"Oh, hey, man, what's up?"

The immediate warmth in his tone makes me sure he's never heard the story about what I did, which again makes me wonder *why*.

"I have a quick question, is this an okay time?"

"Sure is. I'm just going over kitchen plans with Leon."

Leon ... that dude for sure doesn't like me. I'm not sure whether to follow through or quickly hang up, but I assume if I don't make a big deal out of this, it'll probably slip under the radar. Tanner's a sweet guy, but he's the last person to pick up on anything odd.

"Cool, I won't keep you long. Just quickly, does Circus have anything he doesn't eat in particular, or ..."

"He's vegetarian. Why's that?"

"Just plans tonight. Thanks a bunch."

"No worries, Rowan. Catch ya."

I quickly hang up and breathe a sigh of relief. Okay, that went well. I think.

Vegetarian though, huh? Coming from a family whose idea of food is centered around protein, this is going to be a hard one.

I grab my phone and have a look through a few options, before settling on a vegetarian pizza. Grandma makes the best pizzas I've ever tasted, and I know it won't take much to get her help.

The problem is, do I want it?

Am I okay with going to her and asking for help to cook a pizza for a man I literally can't get out of my head?

A man whose body was pressed up against me yesterday, making me want things that are sinful in her eyes?

Again, I'm left at that junction between family and being who I really am.

And I still have no idea which side will win out.

FAKE FRIENDS

CHAPTER NINE
CIRCUS

I could pretend to be out. That's totally a normal thing that normal people do when they invite people over for dinner. Right?

Why did I invite him over?

I'm not opening that can of worms.

All I know is that last night when the loneliness kicked in, I'd been tempted to grab the bottle of scotch from the top of the cupboard that I have reserved for next month.

And I don't want to be that kind of guy.

That scotch is strictly for the anniversary of Mom and Dad's death. The one day a year where I let myself cry and get completely written off.

It's not for me to have a pity party.

Besides, tonight will be all about sharing the photos we took together, and then when the fifty K hits my account, I'll give him his money and he can go.

Easy.

I'll look at it as a goodbye.

The one we never got.

Uh-oh. My thoughts are going there again. To that

wistful place where I imagine how we might have been if he'd stayed.

But he didn't and he's not, and that's the end of that.

Man, I need that drink *more* tonight than I did last night.

I grab my Magic 8-Ball instead and give it a shake. "Should I call tonight off?"

Given I don't have Rowan's number I'm not sure how that would work, but hey, wishful thinking?

Cannot predict now.

Well, fuck you very much.

Since when do sentient objects give you sass?

My doorbell sounds, sending my gut into a spin. Apparently the few hours since I saw him this morning haven't been enough notice for my nerves because now they're going haywire.

I drop my head back and try to school my face back into that I-don't-actually-care expression I'd managed for most of yesterday.

Then I head out to let him in.

I try to look bored even as I picture him all tall and sexy, with that wiry hair that constantly makes him look like he's just been fucked. Even when it's as sweaty as it was this morning.

Scratch that: *especially* when it's as sweaty as it was this morning.

But when I pull open the door, I'm hit with a totally different sight.

"Surprise!" Leon says, holding up a six-pack of beer. "I felt bad about leaving last night, so I decided to stop by and thought we could order takeout."

No, no, no, no, no.

He doesn't wait to be invited in, which isn't something that has ever bothered me before but suddenly does now.

"This is a surprise." I smile, baring all my teeth, and he laughs.

"I thought you'd be happier to see me."

"I didn't think I'd be seeing you at all."

I trail after him toward the kitchen, where he puts the beer in the fridge and pulls one out. "You want?"

"Not right now."

He shrugs and opens the screw top with his forearm. Then he grins at me. Widely.

He's being weird.

I can't quite work out *why*, but he doesn't make a move to do anything other than watch me while he sips from the bottle, and if I didn't know better, I'd say he was waiting for something.

"What's going on with you?" I ask suspiciously.

"Nothing at all. Just wanted to spend time with a friend. Oh—" His eyebrows shoot up like he's just remembered something, but it's not convincing. "You didn't have plans, did you? Shit, and here I've gone and started drinking and everything."

Busted.

But how does he *know*?

"Who told you?"

"Told me what?"

I eye him, trying to work out if he's still shitting me or not, when my doorbell rings again.

His smile widens. "Better get that."

Fucker. Oh yeah, he knows.

And I don't know what game he's playing by showing up, but I don't like it.

When I open the door, and this time Rowan is the one standing there, I suddenly decide that Leon being here is a good thing.

A very good thing.

Maybe even the best thing to ever happen to me.

Because dear God, Rowan looks sexy.

I eye the pizza box he's carrying.

"What's that?"

Maybe asking him to bring dinner was a dumb choice because I forgot to let him know about one tiny thing. The fact I don't eat meat. And knowing Rowan, that thing is going to be packed with animal carcasses.

I step aside and wave him down the hall, not bothering to warn him about Leon's presence. If the way he eyes me when he walks past is any indication, it's probably better he thinks I invited Leon anyway.

The less connection he thinks there is here, the better.

Tonight is going to be fine.

I see the exact moment Rowan realizes we have company. His back tenses and he glances back over his shoulder at me.

"Leon," he says, forcing a friendly tone.

Leon crosses his beefy arms over his chest and forces one word out on a grunt. "Harvey."

Wow. Tonight is going to be a riot.

"Well, it's a good thing I made a large," Rowan says, dropping the pizza box on the counter. He starts opening and closing cupboards at random, making himself at home. It's a weird feeling to have anyone over, let alone two people both equally trying to look more relaxed here than the other.

I have to hold back a laugh.

"So, you two, how was the shoot yesterday?"

Rowan's hand slips from the cupboard door, but he quickly hides his fumble.

"It was fine," I say. "So nice of you to stop by for the viewing."

I catch Leon's eyes, and he does that grin where his lips don't move under his beard, but his eyes crease up at the edges. "Wouldn't miss it for the world."

Total pain in my ass, I swear.

Rowan starts dishing the food onto three plates. "Did Circus tell you it was me?"

"Nope. He put up a photo yesterday, and since I follow that account, I realized it was you straightaway. Not many people in Sunbury with full sleeves."

Rowan's face pales. "Maybe I shouldn't have …"

"Relax, no one in this town knows what I do," I cut in. "Leon's the only one, and it's because we know everything about each other—"

"*Everything*." He pins Rowan with a look.

"*And*," I continue, "he won't say shit. Will you?"

For a rough-looking guy, he pulls off angelic well. "Wouldn't dream of it. After all, Rowan's leaving town soon enough."

Rowan's relaxed expression is long gone. His shoulders are drawn in a tight line, and he slowly closes the pizza box with such care, I swear it's taking up every last brain cell. "You told him?"

"He tells me everything," Leon says, taking another dig.

"Everything …" Rowan repeats. "Let me guess. You know about prom."

"*Is* there something to know?"

I groan loud enough to cut them off. "You guys are pissing me off. Now put your dicks away and let's look at some photos."

Leon stalks over and grabs a plate, looking like he's just won or something, while Rowan actively avoids looking at both of us.

And I don't know why *I* feel guilty, but the hollowness in my gut is hard to shake.

On his way past, Rowan pushes a plate into my hands. A huge slab of pizza and fluffy, light garlic bread. I look closer.

"Is this vegetarian?"

"Well, I'm not going to force you to eat meat, am I?"

Nope, not looking into it. I'm not going to focus on the fact that somehow Rowan took the time to find out what I eat and then clearly cooked it from scratch. Because this is no fast-food pizza. It looks a little like the kind they sell at Harvey's but ... better.

It reminds me of the brownies he used to bake and bring on our outings after I mentioned *once*, at a church bake sale, how good they were.

Or the stupid letters he'd sneak into my backpack after I mentioned a girlfriend did it once and I thought it was kinda cool. Only unlike the girlfriend, his letters weren't full of lyrical prose about how in love with me he was. His were all fart jokes and random thoughts that popped into his head.

I kept them all.

Until I was going through my old room before I sold the house and found them again.

I set every one of those bastards on fire.

It was clearly an emotionally stable year for me.

"Mmm, this pizza is good, city boy." Leon takes another large bite.

"You're welcome, sasquatch."

Leon catches himself before he can laugh, but I'm feeling a bit disconnected from them.

It's weird having people in my house in general.

But I can't help wondering what tonight would have been like if Leon wasn't here. I glance over at Rowan, and he quickly looks away.

Awkward. That's what it would have been.

I sit down and open my laptop. It's already hooked up to the TV I never use.

"Okay, I've edited most of them, but I still have some to go, so any that still have your face in them, don't stress. I know what I'm doing." I keep my voice as flat as possible.

I hit Play and settle back into the couch.

I've spent hours going over these images. Hours of looking at me and Rowan together and trying not to replay any part of yesterday. It was just another shoot. Just another job.

The photos are all out of order now, mostly showing the sequence I edited them in.

And they're hot.

Especially the ones in my studio where we're sharing the same sun lounger. I can feel the way Leon keeps glancing my way, watching my face with each new shot, so I school my features to be neutral, viewing the photos in the analytical way I do when I edit them and not focusing on how they make me feel.

Because that's way too confusing to consider with this kind of attention on me.

The next picture flicks up, and Leon's choke quickly dissolves into a laugh. "Someone was having fun."

Oops, didn't edit that one. In my defense, I didn't think I needed to check for massive boner shots when it was just Rowan and me going through them. And those swimmers do *nothing* to hide the very prominent outline. I'd photoshopped enough of his erections out of the pictures yesterday that I'd needed to jerk off when I was done.

I quickly check Rowan's reaction. I can't read him from the side. "Well, if you know what I did to Circus back in the day, I guess you know why. So you're one of three people who know I'm gay. My reaction shouldn't be much of a surprise."

I almost choke on my pizza. That's the first time I've ever heard that word from him. Even with all our conversations about how much he was struggling, even with all the lust-filled looks he threw my way, he's never come out and called himself gay.

Leon suddenly looks uncomfortable. "Yeah, well. If it helps, I'm not in the business of outing people. You don't need to worry about me."

Rowan nods, not taking his eyes off the screen. "Cool, well, I've seen enough of myself for one night."

I'm hit with the strongest urge to get him to stay. What I do though is watch as he jumps up and rinses his plate, then puts the remaining pizza in my fridge.

"All right, I'm off. Circus, could you send me one or two of those? Preferably sans raging hard-on. Thanks, man. Night, Leon."

Then he's gone so fast I can't even answer him.

We're quiet until we hear the door close.

Leon lets out a long breath as he leans forward and sets his plate on the coffee table. "I hate to say it, but he makes a good pizza."

"What are you doing here?"

"I overheard Tanner on the phone and put two and two together."

"So you came over."

"I know you." He pins me with his most brotherly look. "I care about you. And I know you don't have limits when it comes to him. So while I want to say sorry for showing up here, and I sort of feel like a dick, I'm worried."

"I don't know what you think is going to happen."

"You're telling me if he'd tried to kiss you tonight, you would have stopped it?"

"Yes." *No.* And I hate myself for it.

"You don't need to lie to me. All you need to say is, 'Leon, I'm a pathetic little man who has no control when it comes to Rowan Harvey and his dick.'"

"Ah, but it's been years since I've seen his dick."

Leon snorts and taps my laptop, bringing the image back on screen. "Bitch, *I've* seen his dick after looking at that picture. And I swear to God if little dudes like you two were my type, even I'd want a piece of that."

"Little?" I zoom in on Rowan's chest. "You call that little?"

"Eh. He's got nothing on the men I fuck."

"You scare me."

He laughs and shoves my face. "Real talk. Do you want to fuck him?"

There's no point lying to Leon. "I don't know how to answer that."

"Why? It's a simple question."

"Is it though? Like he said, there are three people who know he's gay, and those three guys were sitting in this room. That's a *lot* of baggage. And the last thing I need is another broken nose."

"Hey, I'm not saying I ship it," he says, holding up his hands. "All I asked about was sex. You don't need to date the guy."

That's true.

"Maybe before he leaves, you two need to get your freaky shit on, and then you'll both have the closure you never got."

"I want to say that's not a terrible idea, but I'm very worried it is."

"Okay, well, you make the call. Do you want me to keep cockblocking you? Or just let this train wreck play out?"

"Why are you assuming it's going to be a train wreck?"

Leon hooks a thumb over his shoulder. "Because news flash. Rowan? Still a mess."

"Yep, no arguments from me. But we both know I'm

a bit of a mess too."

He reaches over and slings an arm around my neck, then presses a whiskery kiss on my head. "Just warn him, if he messes with you again, I'll break his scrawny ass in half."

"Mmhmm." I hold back my smile. "You're a big, bad wolf. We're all so scared."

Leon hangs around for a while and watches a movie before he leaves. I'm itching to check my social media the entire time, but he's put a hard ban on me touching my phone when we're together.

So the minute he's out the front door, I pull out my phone. I have a deposit notification for the fifty thousand, minus my manager's fees, which means the brand must have already started sharing some of the images. I log into my account.

My suspicion is correct.

They have.

And that shit is going crazy.

And because I have zero self-control, I might as well throw gas on this fire.

I go back to the kitchen, pull out the pizza box, and put mine and Leon's used plates in front of it, along with two half-empty beer bottles.

Then I snap a photo.

Dinner and nights in with him.
This time, I even add a love heart.

CHAPTER TEN
ROWAN

I've been back in Sunbury for over a month, and already the shifts at Harvey's are wearing thin. I have no interest in taking over from my parents; I assume that'll be down to Piper. She loves it here and did an online business certificate instead of running off to college like I did.

In order to stop working here though, I either need to leave again or find something else to fill my time.

Still working on what that might be.

I finish grilling the beef patty in front of me and slide it onto a burger with all the toppings. One of the options we don't have here is a vegetarian menu, and it makes me wonder if that's the reason Circus never comes in and maybe it doesn't have anything to do with me at all.

Okay, I'm not a dumb shit. I know it has to do with me, but at least I don't think that's the only reason.

Since noticing that, I'm beginning to wonder if it's something we should do though.

Circus can't be the only vegetarian in town, and maybe it's not a large clientele, but it might mean those people and their friends choose to come here instead of

Peg's sometimes. Our business is solid, but would doing something a little different make it even better?

Mom and Dad are set in their ways, but maybe it's something I can run past Piper.

Circus clearly enjoyed that pizza last night. And if we're already making them from scratch, where's the harm?

I glance up at the clock just as it ticks over to 5:00 p.m., and two of the part-timers leave the break room and enter the kitchen.

The high school kids spend more time messing around than making the food, but at least I don't have to deal with their hormonal asses.

I hang up my apron, shove a baseball cap down over my sweaty hair, and leave.

But when I get out front, Piper stops me.

"He's been waiting for you for half an hour."

Circus is in a booth up the back, playing with his phone.

"Thanks."

I'd thought last night was a solid fuck-you when I showed up to find Leon there. He clearly didn't want to be alone with me, despite inviting me over, so what the hell is he doing here now?

I slide into the booth opposite him. "Pleasant surprise."

A broad smile crosses his face, but he keeps staring at his screen. "Have you seen this?"

"What?"

"Holy shit." He laughs and slides the phone toward me.

I don't know what I'm looking at. "*Who is him?*" I read. "That's bad grammar."

"They're looking for you."

"What?" I don't know why he's smiling.

"Relax, there's no way for them to find you. I checked. We have no social media friends in common, even on my normal page, *and* I hide all the people I follow anyway. They're looking for a needle in a haystack."

I shift uncomfortably and glance around the diner. It's past the afternoon rush, and I'm unsure whether that's a good thing. Less people are around to overhear, but it makes the room quiet, and I'm conscious our voices will carry.

"Come on." I go outside and Circus follows me. "Now, explain what's going on?"

"The last few days I've been posting pictures of us captioning them with dumb stuff and always calling you 'him.'"

I know. I've seen. But of course I don't mention that. "And now people want to know who I am?"

"Yep. This worked out way better than I thought it would. When *Royal Swimwear* first noticed people asking about who you were, they ran with it. Everything they post is hashtag him. Circus and him. They're pushing the secret angle, and it's driving people nuts that they can't find you."

My mouth won't close. "Why the hell do they care who some random guy in a bunch of photos with you is?"

"This is the kicker. They think we're dating. See, there's this whole subculture online of people shipping certain influencer couples. And the ones who follow some of the gay couples out there are next-level supporters. Today, the brand's post was 'You and him deserve to be Royal. Show us your Royalty' and people have been posting pictures with their boyfriends all day."

"Us? Dating?" My brain feels stuck.

"Trust me when I say I would have preferred literally anyone else to do this with me. But you're it. And if we play up this fake dating angle …"

I feel like I've been dropped into an alternate universe or something. "Won't people be mad when they find out the truth?"

"Nope. Because they won't. You want to stay hidden, and I never once mentioned we were dating. People put that together themselves."

"Because you baited them into it."

He laughs. "Maybe a little."

Oh, man, I have a bad feeling about this. "The more popular this thing is, the more chance someone we know will see it." And the thought of someone in my family seeing those shots? Panic starts to claw at my throat. "Fuck, maybe this was a bad idea."

"Whoa, calm down."

"Calm *down*?" Sure, that's easy for him to say. "This is exactly the sort of thing I never wanted to happen." My voice is getting louder, but I've lost all control over it.

"I'll stop posting, then." Circus glares up at me from under his dark lashes. "Don't stress about it. No more sneaky shots of the two of us. No more posts. Relax. I'll build my audience without you."

"It's not …" God, how do I even begin to describe to him the sheer panic I have about my family starting to question anything to do with my sexuality? I've kept it hidden for so long because none of them have assumed I'm anything other than straight. I quickly glance around. "I'm still in the closet for a reason. I love my family, I don't want them to disown me."

"Well, maybe you can share your little secret once you've moved away from here."

Ah. That. I shuffle my feet and stare down the other end of the road. "What if … what if you kept the money, and I stayed here?"

"What?"

"I don't want to leave, Circus. I'm sorry. I know that was our deal, and I loved the time I spent in Portland, but when I picture my life, I picture myself living *here*. Traveling maybe. Coming and going, but this is my home. This is where my family is. Are you really going to make me leave them?"

"You mean the awesome family who doesn't even

know the real you? The horror! I'm such an asshole."

"They're stuck in their ways."

"They're homophobes."

I grit my teeth because he's right and I don't want to argue. But it hurts to be reminded of the fact the people I love unconditionally have definite conditions in return.

He steps a bit closer and drops his voice. "I'm being a dick. I get it. But you're gay, dude. And that's not a bad thing to be. I fucking hate that they've convinced you it is."

I study the bump in his nose again. "Since when do you care anyway?"

Circus quickly backs up. "I don't. Deal with your own shit. Like I said, I'll go back to only sharing my pretty face with the world. Oh, and that money came through. I'll send through your share once I'm home."

I guess that's his way of telling me he still wants me gone.

I know he can't technically banish me or anything like that, but the problem is that if I stay, Circus knows too much. It would be too easy for him to let slip one night that I'm the one who broke his nose five years ago and that's the reason I left town.

Because getting that out there is going to start the questions of *why*. Why were we alone that night? Why did I punch him? Why didn't Circus tell anyone until now?

And actually, I'd kind of like to know the answer to

that one as well.

But I can't bring myself to ask.

"Circus ..."

He waits. Gives me a chance to answer. But my throat feels stuck, and all the rampant thoughts set loose in my brain refuse to come out.

I sigh and my focus lands on his nose again. "I really *am* sorry."

"Sorry ..." He closes the distance between us, and for the first time since we've reconnected, he meets my eyes and I get a glimpse of the guy I fell for. "The sad part is, Rowan, you're *still* apologizing for the wrong thing."

He's gone before I can even *begin* to figure out what he means.

That night, Circus follows through on his word.

Except when I log in to my bank account and see almost double the amount we agreed on, I'm sure there must be a mistake.

A text quickly follows it.

Unknown: *They were so happy, they paid us double. Here's your share minus fees. Thanks for helping. C.*

Fuck.

I sink down on the side of my bed, staring at all those digits. Is this real life?

I've never seen this much money ever, and suddenly

it's all sitting in my bank account. Were the pictures really *that* good?

I hunch forward, head between my knees, and let my phone drop to the ground.

Jesus.

Who the hell has a panic attack over *having* money?

My phone stares back at me, the message he sent dulled, and the dumbest, strangest, most absurd thought starts to kick around in my head.

Me: *I think I have a deal for you*

CHAPTER ELEVEN
Circus

I kick at the dirt, wondering how long I should give him before I decide he won't show. There's still five minutes until our agreed meeting time, but if he wanted to be here, he would be already. So I figure a minute past is a hard limit.

Because I'm an understanding kind of guy.

I inhale the smell of damp forest and wallflower just as a car turns onto the road leading to the parking lot. I want to be disappointed he showed up.

I'm not.

I nod in acknowledgment like meeting with an ex-friend is all totally cool and how I normally spend the weekends.

Crown Trails is busier today than it normally is during the week, and with the arrival of spring, more people from across the state drive up here for a day out. There's a park with benches and grills for families to use, right before the entrance to a few different trail heads.

"You're early," he says, jumping out of the car and throwing a backpack on. He's wearing the same hat he was the other day, and his eyes are bright in the shadow from its brim.

"Are you going to tell me what we're doing here yet?" I ask as he locks the car and approaches.

"Figured we could take a hike. For old times."

I'm confused. "I'm sorry, are we friends again? Why the hell would you think I'd want to do that?"

He leans in and I hurry to back up a step. "Because we're fake dating, remember? Should probably get shots of us doing things together."

Did I take a knock to the head? Rowan heads for the path, and I scramble to follow him. "Fake dating?"

Am I hearing this right?

"That's what I wanted to talk to you about. But first, usual spot. Then I'll tell you my plan."

The usual spot? Of course he wants to take me to the one spot in all of Crown Trails that I actively avoid. I'm also not loving the familiarity in his voice.

Rowan walks ahead of me, and as I watch each step, I'm transported back in time to when he was a little shorter and a little leaner and his arms were free of ink.

He throws a smile back over his shoulder, and it's exactly the same smile as the one that, back then, I would have done anything for.

Not today, Satan.

We've walked this path so many times together that even all these years later it's instinctual. The way one of us will pause to let the other pass when the path gets narrow, or the steep inclines we help each other over.

And then we reach the lookout. It's mostly overgrown with shrubbery now, but there's still a rocky ledge where we used to sit and flirt and talk about the dumbest shit, just so we could be together.

During senior year, that was literally all I ever wanted.

Rowan sets down his backpack and sits on the left of the ledge, hanging his legs over the side.

Do I join him and try to recreate whatever kind of something he's clearly pushing for?

Or do I keep my stubborn ass over here and pretend like I'm totally unfazed.

Because this complete time warp is doing nothing to clarify my feelings for him.

I stay standing.

Rowan lets out a short chuckle when he sees me cross my arms and lean back against the rock wall. "Fair enough."

"Ready to talk yet?"

He unzips his backpack and pulls a container from inside. If that's what I think it is …

Brownies.

So he's not here to play fair, then.

"I should never have forgiven you, you know."

"I know." He catches my eyes. "I still haven't forgiven myself, if that helps? And after spending a good part of my life regretting what happened, I can promise it's not something that will ever happen again. Not that I expect you to believe me."

"I don't."

"Good. You're still smart." He turns and looks out over the valley below.

Smart is debatable. Academically, I'm okay; emotionally, I'm an absolute dumbshit, because while I stand here and watch him, I'm trying to justify moving closer.

It's not like it would *hurt* anything, right?

And I've already said I forgive him for what happened. If there's anything Mom taught me it's not to offer forgiveness lightly, because once it's given, you lose all rights to throwing that thing back in their face.

I remind myself of Leon's advice. Maybe I *do* need to fuck this thing out of my system.

Given Rowan is still closeted, I know that shit is unlikely, but maybe his advice is close?

Maybe I just need to give myself permission and see where this shitshow leads.

After all, at this point is it even possible to be any more emotionally screwed up than I am already?

At least this time I have the heads-up he's leaving.

That reminder is the excuse I need to move forward and take the place beside him.

Let's burn this thing to the ground, shall we?

I grab a brownie, and it's possible I've forgotten how good these bastards are, or maybe Rowan's gotten even better at cooking since I last had one, but the chocolate melts in my mouth.

"Oh *God*. Am I drooling? I think I'm drooling."

"Can confirm there's no drool."

I nudge the container toward him. "Well, go on. I can't be the only piggy out here."

"Nah, they're all yours." He pats the tank top over his toned stomach. "With no gym in Sunbury, I have to keep an eye on this."

I consider offering to keep an eye on it for him. Or his ass? I could *definitely* keep a close eye on that. See? I'm a generous guy.

"Is that how you got so ripped? The gym?"

"Yep, I love working out." He flashes me a quick smile. "Good to see you noticed."

"There was a lot I couldn't help noticing about you the other day."

"Yeah, and you were so impressed, you let people think we were dating."

"Total marketing move."

"As long as you believe that."

And like, I'm 99 percent sure he's messing around, but I'm also low-key worried I've been *that* obvious. "Well, I'm not the one who said they have a deal."

"Ah." He shifts a little. "Yeah, that. So I'll begin by saying this was a completely random thought, but I actually think it would work out for both of us."

"Listening."

Rowan turns, tucking a foot under the leg still

hanging over the cliff wall, and faces me. "Like I said the other day, I don't want to go anywhere."

"You're going back on your word. I'm shocked."

"If you still want me to leave after I've said my piece—" He takes a deep breath. "—I will. That was our deal, and thanks to us getting paid extra, I'm set up to do it."

It's my turn to shift. Us getting paid more? Total lie. But the last thing I need is more money, and he could clearly use it. Anything to get him out from relying on his family.

"And what makes you think you can change my mind?"

"You said you've been getting a lot of attention because people think you're dating some mystery dude, right?"

"*Him.* Yes. Total heartthrob, who I'm apparently madly in love with."

"Well, that wasn't always untrue."

"Lucky I refined my judgment."

Rowan slides the tray of brownies away—rude!—and shifts a bit closer. "You know, I lost count of the number of times I almost kissed you up here."

Whoa. I swallow. "If you'd given me even the smallest sign, I would have mauled you like a bear."

"Noted." He reaches across me, and I almost suffocate on air as he reaches into my pocket and pulls out my phone. He leans his weight onto one arm behind me and lifts my phone with the other. "You'll need to shut that pretty mouth of yours."

He's right. Gaping is not a good look. I play along, because what the hell, tilting my head so he can press his face to my shoulder. The hat completely covers him.

Rowan takes the photo and hands my phone back.

"I thought you didn't want any more photos?" I ask cautiously.

"That's my deal. You be okay with me staying, and I'll give you whatever sort of boyfriendly shots you like."

Oh, that's so, so tempting.

I ended up deleting the photo I posted of myself last night because all people wanted to know was where my boyfriend was. That's not the kind of attention I'm interested in, but if I give the people what they want ...

"I thought you were worried about your family finding out?"

"Oh, man, I'm terrified of that. But the thing is, I can deny it. Tell them I'm just taking the photos to make some cash, and I have the bank balance to prove it. They still won't be happy, but at least they won't be worried for my soul."

I purse my lips. "Still not planning on coming out, then?"

"I guess one day, when my grandparents move on and my parents get older, I might try it out then. But the little voices in my head are hard to shake."

"And have you? Tried to shake them?"

"Are you asking if I've hooked up with anyone?"

I cringe. "You know what, I'm not sure I want to know."

"Relax. There have been a couple of weak moments in clubs, but other than that, I've kept it securely in my pants."

"That sounds fucking tragic."

He doesn't look at me as he manages a sad smile. "Yeah, I know. And the shitty thing is not being able to talk to anyone about it."

"But you've obviously come to terms with it? That you're gay?"

"Yeah. It took a lot of time. I went to a meeting for a conversion therapy group, talked to people about how it worked, and met with some guys who had successful experiences. I didn't end up going through with it, but that was me at my darkest. Then I saw a psychologist for a little while. She helped me get to the label and said a lot of gay men grow up with the same issues I have." He pauses, looking awkward. "And I talked about you a lot. She's the one who suggested that maybe I needed closure in order to move on."

"Did it work?"

He looks at me, stare tracing my features. "I don't know yet."

It's a good reminder that this thing between us ended for a reason. As much as I want to throw out all the hypotheticals of what might have been, the only certainty is that Rowan never would have come out, so it never would have worked.

He clears his throat. "What did you mean the other day? About apologizing for the wrong thing?"

Ah, that. A moment where I completely lost my mind and shared more than I should have. I'm about to brush aside the ridiculousness of it all when I glimpse his serious face. "Just ..." I swallow. "It was never my nose I was angry about."

"What—"

"You left." My voice gets louder than I mean it to. "And how fucked-up is that? I was ready to forgive you, *that exact second*, for what you did, but you left before I could. You cut all ties, and I ... I thought I'd never get to see you again. *That's* the part that hurt."

Rowan doesn't answer. I have no idea how he's processing my reaction to this huge event he's had hanging over his head for half a decade, but I can't find the emotional energy to be any more real with him than I already have been.

He shakes his head. "You wanted me to stay?"

"I did. At the time. I guess that's what stupid teenage hormones do to a guy."

"Yeah. I guess."

"Well, it doesn't bother me either way now," I say, forcing a happier tone. "I've got myself an on-demand boyfriend *without* benefits, and you get to stick around here."

Rowan's smile looks forced. "Without benefits? Damn, hey?"

"You can talk big all you like, but we both know you're not ready to put your money where your mouth is."

His shoulders slump. "True."

And he looks so dejected, I can't help but reach over and give his thigh a quick squeeze. "One day things will be different."

Rowan's large, tattooed hand covers mine. "God, I hope so."

CHAPTER TWELVE
ROWAN

Every time I'm with Circus, we go somewhere different. Who would have thought that Oregon had so many cool sights to see? He seems to know all the areas that have the best light, or the best backdrop, and I'm slowly slipping into that place where he occupies my mind ninety percent of the time.

Which isn't great when I'm working the grill at Harvey's or helping Grandma out in the kitchen.

The difference now though is whenever those thoughts come up, I don't immediately push them out. Instead, I try to remind myself that it's normal, there's nothing wrong with who I am and who I'm attracted to.

And I've always been attracted to Circus.

His confession on Crown Trails left me reeling and opened up a whole load of questions about what life would have been like if I'd stayed here. Would we have gotten through it? Would I have ever come out?

I know that both of those scenarios are unlikely, but I keep torturing myself with them anyway.

Still, knowing that things could have been different makes me more grateful for the time we have now.

He's been loosening up too. Less of the tense anger directed at me and more smiles, more casual touches even when the camera isn't on us.

The problem is though, Circus only wants to meet up once or twice a week, take a range of photos, and then he posts those over the next few days.

I get it. This whole thing isn't real, and the more pictures he takes, the more interactions, and the more followers ... all that stuff.

He's smart about the way he runs his brand or whatever, and by packing as much work into a day or two as possible, he frees up the rest of the week for whatever else he has planned.

Those plans just don't happen to involve me.

I'm halfway to Leita's place when my phone starts to ring, and Circus's name shows up on the screen. I'm not proud of how quickly I hurry to answer it.

"Hey, what's up?" I ask, definitely not hoping this call is for us to hang out or anything like that, because I know what's up with us. I'm not deluded.

"The weirdest thing just happened ..." His voice sounds distracted.

"Oh yeah?"

"Yeah. I was sent a box of clothes for *us*. The brand didn't even give my manager a heads-up which is strange. I've never heard of the brand, but ... their clothes are pretty sweet."

"Awesome. I'm heading to my sister's, but I can

come over once I'm done. It'll probably be a couple of hours though."

He doesn't answer right away. "What are you doing there?"

"Babysitting my nephews. My brother-in-law works long days, so I watch the kids once or twice a week so she can head to the gym in Port Welling."

"Well ... do you want company?"

My gut flips with the offer. This is the first time since I've been back that Circus has actively requested we hang out, and it has nothing to do with his work. At least, I'm assuming it doesn't. He'd have to know I wouldn't let him post pictures of my nephews online.

"I'd love that." Maybe I should have asked Leita first, or told him just to wait until I came around, but considering I didn't think I'd get to see him at all today, I got ahead of myself.

"Cool. I'll ride over."

"You need an address?"

He laughs. "You're back in Sunbury, princess. I know the place."

We hang up and I jog the rest of the street to get to Leita's place, wanting to make sure she has the heads-up before he gets there.

"I thought you'd never show," Leita says, grabbing her workout bag the second I'm through the door.

I smile. "I thought Piper was supposed to be the impatient one?"

"Only on my good days. Now, you're okay? There's lunch ready in the fridge for when they get hungry."

I strap the baby carrier to my chest. "I got this. But, ah …"

She narrows her eyes at me. "Ah, what? Please don't tell me you need me back early …"

"No, nothing like that. Just, you remember Circus?"

"Yeah. I know Circus."

"He was going to come over too, if that's okay?"

She laughs. "What, are you guys friends again?"

"Ah, yes?"

"Aww, that's cute. I know Dad didn't like him, but he made you less of a dumbass jock when he was around."

"Well, eff you very much."

"Uncle Rowan!" My nephew comes tearing out of the living area and slams into my legs.

"And that's my cue." Leita ducks out the front door before anyone has a chance to stop her.

"Okay, Jase, ready to go outside?"

By the time Circus arrives, I've got baby Blake in the carrier, and I'm kicking a ball to Jason and Levi. Circus slows his bike, then lifts the camera slung around his neck and takes a photo.

"No posting that," I warn him when he's close enough to hear me.

"Fucking duh."

"And no swearing."

"Oops. I forgot that's a thing with kids, isn't it?"

"Most of them."

We kick the ball back and forth a few times, then head inside to feed the boys. Jason and Levi sit at the table stuffing their faces like the ravenous monsters they are, and Circus watches on while I give Blake his bottle.

"I want that," he eventually says.

"Want what? To feed him?"

"No, *kids*. Lots of kids. I want a big family someday."

I study him for a moment, but his gaze doesn't shift from Blake. "Does that mean you'll end up marrying a woman?"

Circus scowls. "What the—*what*? No. I don't know who I'm going to marry, but I won't be choosing based on reproductive parts. This isn't *The Handmaid's Tale*, you creep."

I laugh. "But wouldn't it be easier that way? Man, if I could be attracted to anyone I wanted, I would definitely choose to fall for a woman."

Circus slowly lowers himself onto his stool, and this time I have his attention. "Is that how you think it works?"

"Doesn't it?"

"Well, you tell me. How does it feel when you meet someone you're instantly attracted to? Or even someone who you grow an attraction to over time? Do you go out looking specifically for someone to meet a certain criteria, or does it just happen?"

"It just happens."

"It's exactly the same for me, man. Sorry to break it to you, but I can't force myself to fall for any one gender, just like you can't force yourself to be straight."

I sigh and pretend to be checking the bottle. "I've tried, you know. To be straight."

His lips flatten. "I'm not surprised. And how did that go for you?"

"Not ... well." I cringe when I remember the massive shit fight I left behind in Portland. Walking away was the right thing to do, but I probably could have handled ending my relationship better.

"Sorry, I guess. I still don't think you should be trying to change who you are, just to make other people happy."

"You've made your thoughts on the whole thing very clear."

My tone makes it obvious the conversation is over. And as much as I'd be happy to sit here and talk about anything with Circus, there are only so many times I can rehash how my family feels. I'm trying, so hard, to leave all those bad thoughts and negative images behind me. I'm trying to shake the voice. But every time I'm reminded of why those thoughts exist in the first place, it brings them back stronger.

I want to enjoy my time with Circus, without the homophobic thoughts poisoning it.

We spend a couple of hours at Leita's, before we walk back to my place to get my car. Thankfully no one seems to be home, or at least not around to question where I'm going and who with. I strap Circus's bike to the roof and drive us both back to his place in the forest.

I still can't get over the size of it.

The big family thing sort of explains why he'd want so much room, but surely when partners and offspring come into the equation, he'll be looking to move back closer to town. I wasn't joking when I asked him if he got scared—that wall of glass overlooking the valley is exactly the sort of setup a serial killer would love to exploit.

When we get inside, I grab a glass of water and follow Circus into the studio. There's a large box on the floor with a whole bunch of colorful material spilling over the top.

"What is that?" I ask, holding up a tie-dyed tank top.

"Mine." He snatches it from me. "I'm sure there were matching shorts in here somewhere." And true to his word, he pulls out a pair a moment later.

"You're going to wear those?"

"Hell yeah, they're awesome." He pulls his shirt over his head, putting all that warm brown skin on display for me, before pulling the tank top on. And of course, if anyone can pull it off, it's him.

The rest of the selection follows a similar kind of hippy theme. Beads and tassel vests and earthy colors.

"Here." Circus hands over a brown leather vest and flowy animal-print pants.

"You're shitting me, right?"

"Definitely not." He crosses his arms, and I don't know when he changed his shorts, but I *am* sorry I missed it. "They'll look hot."

Hot? Well who am I to be arguing with that? He doesn't let me pull on an undershirt, so my chest is on full display, and I'm hyperaware of the way Circus shamelessly drinks me in as I strip. I might even flex accidentally-on-purpose to really give him a show.

"In the chair."

I do as I'm told, relatively used to this by now. He fusses with my hair and starts to roll up a bandana that he wraps around my head and ties at the back.

"I look like I'm wearing a sweatband."

"That's the point." He circles me, fussing with my hair some more, and when he steps directly in front of me, leaning forward so he can make the thing sit right, I'm swamped with his scent. Something manly and spicy that makes me want to lean forward and press my nose into his chest.

"Okay, that's good."

"How have your posts been going this week?"

"Good. Loads of people still asking when I'm going to show your face. They're starting to think you're butt ugly." He throws a grin my way. "Not far from the truth."

I pat the back of his head. "We both know you think I'm hot as fuck." I'm only joking, and I fully expect for him to tell me to piss off, but ...

"I guess I can't deny it, when it's never been a

secret."

Hmm … *hello*. That's a massive step up from pain in the ass, so I'll definitely take it.

Circus has set up some kind of desert backdrop, with a wooden deck floor and twinkle lights overhead. There's a fold-out wooden chair and animal skin rug, which I'm going to assume is fake. Given Circus's aversion to eating animals, I can't see him decorating his house with them.

"I figured you can sit in the chair, pretending to look out at the view, and I'll sit on the rug facing the camera."

"Will that work?"

"I know what I'm doing."

Well, that's true. The guy knows how to take a good photo. I sit like the good dog I am, and Circus takes his position. When he's in front of the camera, he's like another person. So charismatic, I can't look away.

He loops one arm around my calf and gives the camera such a sexy pout, I have to remind myself to turn, before my face wrecks the shot. We take a few more, each shot getting more creative with ways he can make it look good without getting any of my recognizable features in the frame.

Circus flicks through a few of the photos on his camera. "Okay, back in the chair, I want to try something."

I'm like his little puppet with the way I so obediently follow what he says. And as soon as my ass hits the seat, Circus hands me his phone.

"These are two influencers I've been following for a while now. They started around the same time as me and then they teamed up. I have no idea if they're actually dating, but these guys are the shit. They get modeling contracts and advertising campaigns and all the good stuff."

I take his phone and flick through a few of the posts. My first thought is that these guys are hot. *Really* hot. I pause over a picture where one of the guys is biting the other's lip ... and they're both naked. All I can see is one of their asses, but I start getting warm around the neck. I scroll a little slower, studying each of them.

And while none of them are overtly sexual, they're all a hell of a lot sexier than anything we've taken.

"I can't help but think there's a big difference between their stuff and ours," I say.

"You can see both their faces."

Well yeah, there's that too. And I have to admit, their expressions are one of the biggest draws. It's hard to believe they're not actually dating when they look at each other like that. "You know my rule," I remind him.

"I know. I want to see how we can create something like that while keeping you secret."

Something like ... that. Okay. So my whole plan was to deny anything gay if my parents saw these photos, but if we're taking the sex factor up a notch, that's going to be borderline impossible.

I clear my throat. "Okay."

What's that? I have zero self-control?

There's no arguing with that assessment when Circus climbs into my lap. I inhale deeply, trying to steel myself against the war of loathing and lust fighting for space in my mind. My hands are dying to reach out and touch, but I'm not sure where the lines are here. I'm not sure if the lines exist at all.

Circus cups my neck, and the look he gives me steals my breath away. He's far enough back that his face will be in the shot, but it's closer than we've been in a long time, and when those deep gray eyes meet mine ... I'm a goner.

"What's the matter, scared?" His expression is challenging.

I lick my lips and reach up to run my knuckles over his cheek. See? I can do this. Every other time it's been all Circus touching me, him directing me what to do.

This time he's making me initiate.

He leans into my touch, closing his eyes, and something in my chest gives a little pang. I know this is all for the camera, but when you've imagined getting this close to a man for the entirety of your adult life, apparently your body doesn't get the message.

So I do what I've always imagined doing.

I grab his hip, then let my hand slide up his back, over the top of his shirt. It's all hard muscle under my palm and I have to cup his face with my other hand to stop it from shaking.

"You okay?" he asks. The natural rasp to his voice encourages my cock to thicken faster.

"I don't know."

"We can stop."

We probably should before that voice can kick in and tell me everything I'm doing is wrong, but I shake my head instead.

"You know, if you started your own account, you'd be able to get your own sponsorships, build your own brand. It would mean when we stop doing this, you'll be able to keep making money from it."

"Seems too risky."

"You can keep it anonymous. Even brand it with all the *him* stuff we've been doing. Literally no one in town has my account except Leon, so what's the chances they'd find yours?"

That's true. But still, this is pushing it enough.

"You more than keep me on my toes."

His gaze drops to my crotch, and a smile spreads over his face. "You seem to like it."

"Yeah," I whisper. "No complaints here."

He shifts closer and wraps his arms around my neck.

I struggle to breathe.

He's so close. So fucking beautiful.

I run a finger over his defined jawline, wishing this was real, and wishing I could take the moment further.

"You know how I avoid the boner issue?" he asks.

"Hmm?" My thoughts are getting slower, and that

slimy feeling is starting to set in. That inherent wrongness that cloaks everything masculine in my life makes me want to throw Circus off my lap and leave.

I refuse to let it win.

My hands grip his back tighter, and I force myself to meet his eyes.

"What do you do?"

"I jerk off."

I don't know what look I'm wearing, but it must be hilarious because he starts to laugh.

"Relax, man. You can't tell me you don't do it."

"Not ... not often."

"What?"

"Well ... guys are what turns me on, and thinking about guys makes me feel uncomfortable, so ..." Dear God, stop talking. This is way more information than Circus ever needs to know.

"Do *I* make you uncomfortable?"

"What?"

"Do I—" He leans in and nips my ear. "Make you. Feel uncomfortable?"

"No."

"And you've done work on learning how to accept yourself, right?"

"Yes ..."

"Then let's do some more."

"Like ...?"

He pulls back and locks eyes with mine. "As soon as

you're home, call me."
"What ... why?"
"Just trust me."

CHAPTER THIRTEEN
Circus

Well, look at me being an absolute saint by trying to help Rowan release some tension.

Sitting on his lap like that and seeing his pupils blown out with lust cemented the fact that I need closure. So *maybe* this is somewhat selfish. Maybe. A little, I guess.

There's absolutely no harm in him popping a boner during our shoots because I can edit those beasts right out, but ... well, first, I hate the thought he's still struggling with his sexuality. That shit isn't cool. It makes me want to confront his homophobic family and tell them all to go to hell.

How anyone can claim to be Catholic and have a problem with who people fall in love with is beyond me.

And second ... he's just so. Hot.

I've *needed* to jerk off before our shoots because otherwise I'd be dry humping him like an animal.

So it only made sense to suggest we jerk off together ... but separately.

Because maybe if he gets comfortable with this, he'll get comfortable with *other stuff*.

"You ready?" I say, tilting my head toward my phone.

He blows out an exhale. "I'm not sure about this."

I smile at where my phone is sitting on my bedside table. "We can do it on video if that's easier?"

"Nope, baby steps."

It was worth a try. Knowing Rowan is lying on his bed, preparing to jerk himself off, has me straining the front of my briefs. "It's okay, you know. Forget all the negative shit you've been told. I have no idea what it's like obviously, but I *do* know that thinking about guys isn't bad. It's hot as fuck. Tight abs, round pecs, thick thighs ..."

He breathes heavily into the phone.

Knowing he's turned on makes me want to take more risks. I push my underwear down roughly. "Want to know what I'm doing now?" My voice goes husky as I wrap my hand around my erection and give it a solid stroke.

"Yes."

"I'm holding my cock."

"Fuck ..." There's movement on the other side. "What else?"

"You really want to know?"

He hesitates, but only for a second. "Yes, please, keep going."

Well, phone sex isn't exactly what I had in mind, but who am I to say no to it?

"Grab your cock."

"Already have."

Ooh, that's a hot image. Tatted hands wrapped around his long dick. "Good, squeeze it tight for me." I give myself a good few pumps. "Fuck, I'm so hard."

His breathing is getting deeper, and if I had to guess, I'd say his phone is right next to his ear. It makes sense, not wanting *this* conversation overheard.

"It feels good," I tell him. "So good. Are you still stroking yourself?"

"Yes."

"Tell me."

"I ... I'm hard too. It's ... nrg, it's been so long."

"Are you leaking?"

He grunts.

"Tell me."

"Yes ..." His voice is so shaky it makes me wonder if I'm pushing this thing too far. We were just supposed to mutually jerk off, and then I was going to talk him down from a freak-out afterward. This is ... screw it, I'm all in.

I slide my thumb over the tip. "God, I'm leaking so much. Hearing your voice, knowing you're touching yourself, it's such a fucking turn-on. Cup your balls. Squeeze them."

He grunts again and I'm sure he's following through.

I reach down and do the same. "Mine are so tight. My dick is *throbbing*."

His breath hitches and I'd put money down that he's

close. I start to stroke myself in earnest, imagining him here, lying next to me. Watching those tattooed arms flex while he strokes himself. I can just picture his parted lips, his screwed-up eyes ... running my tongue over his abs.

"Faster. Stroke faster."

I can hear him. The slick of his hand moving over his cock starts to fill the phone, and I speed up to match the rhythm. I slam my eyes closed and picture him rolling over and covering my body, hand closing over my dick as he beats me off.

Fuck ...

"I'm coming." The words have barely left my mouth before my balls tighten and unleash. My cock throbs with each spurt of cum that hits my stomach and chest, and I stroke myself through the high.

Rhythmic panting fills my ear, and then Rowan lets out a low groan. It's possibly the hottest sound I've heard in a long time, until ...

He sniffs, breath hitching on an inhale, and this time when he starts to pant, it's not the sexy kind.

That snaps me out of my orgasm high.

"Shit, are you okay?" I hurry to sit up, ignoring the sticky mess all down the front of me.

There's no answer, but he hasn't hung up.

I have no idea what's happening in his head, but I can tell by the way he's breathing that he's holding back tears.

"This was nothing out of the ordinary," I tell him. "You didn't touch me, I didn't touch you. We're just two friends who jerked off completely separately." Still no answer. And shit, I'm not qualified for this. Do I suggest he talks to someone? Will that make his issues worse?

And it's not like he can have that kind of conversation in his tiny house anyway.

"Okay, here's the plan," I say, talking out of my ass. "Right now, you're going to answer me. Anything. Just one word. I don't care if you're crying or whatever."

"I'm not fucking crying."

"Perfect, good talk. Next, you're going to grab some tissues and clean up."

"I don't have tissues."

"A shirt, then."

He sniffs loudly. "Gran does the laundry. I don't want—"

"Not for this, she doesn't. Now listen. You're going to grab a shirt, wipe yourself down, then pack a bag. You're coming over, and we'll watch a movie or some shit, I don't know. We're going to do something completely normal and basic that you'd do with anyone, and I'm going to prove to you that this doesn't have to be weird."

"Circus, I—"

"Nope. I don't want to hear excuses. I've told you what to do. Now repeat it back. What's first?"

I have no clue if getting my bossy on will help

anything, but I figure he's been listening to others for so long, maybe he needs a positive voice to take over until he can do it for himself.

"I'm grabbing a shirt. And wiping myself off."

"Perfect. Just like after any old jerk-off. You haven't done anything special. Now what's next?"

"Umm ..." His voice is starting to sound normal again. "A bag. I'm packing a—wait. *Why* am I packing a bag?"

I tear a bunch of tissues out of the box and start to wipe myself down, not sure whether to give the real answer. "Because I'm not an asshole. You clearly need a bit of extra help tonight, and I have a big house. We'll hang out until you feel better, then you have the pick of bedrooms."

He laughs lightly. "What about yours?"

"Oh, honey. If I thought you'd share a bed with me for a minute, I'd bother answering that question."

He laughs softly, but it cuts straight off. "I don't want to feel like this."

"How do you feel?"

"Disgusting. Embarrassed. Ashamed."

I frown, trying to picture a time where jerking off doesn't leave me feeling relaxed and happy. I can't let him dwell on it. "You're not packing."

Noise picks up on the other end as he moves around. "Okay, done."

"I'll see you in ten minutes. And, Rowan, don't keep

me waiting."

***

Fifteen minutes later, and I start getting the sneaky impression he's not coming. Half an hour later, and I'm convinced.

I want to get angry, but really, I'm just sad. Sad that his family has messed with him so much he can't even enjoy a few solo minutes of pleasure. I'm torn between calling him and leaving him alone because I have no idea what to do in this situation.

I never had that massive existential crisis when it came to my sexuality. I don't know if that's because I knew Mom and Dad wouldn't care, or if it's because I've literally never viewed it as one way or another. Being pansexual, I'm open to meeting anyone. When it comes to the future love of my life, I have no preferences other than them loving me as much as I plan to love them. My parents set an example on what a family should feel like, and I plan on giving all of that and more to mine.

The crunch of gravel outside makes my head shoot up, and I swear I see headlights in the hall to the foyer. I'm smiling before I leave my living room, and when I finally get to the front door and open it, Rowan is waiting.

His eyes are red.

"I almost thought you were going to chicken out."

He laughs and I get a quick glimpse of his gorgeous smile. "I did. And then I didn't. And then I did again. And now I'm here. Better let me in before my mind changes again."

I step aside and Rowan passes me, heading straight for the living room. He dumps his bag and then sits down, burying his hands into his hair.

I chuckle as I join him. "Maybe we should have started off simpler. A couple of rounds of gay porn, before working up to phone sex."

He jolts and looks up at me. "We had phone sex."

It's not a question. The disbelief in his tone makes me feel a little bad that we didn't have the whole limits conversation beforehand. "Did I overstep?"

"Definitely not. It was ..." His voice dips. "Amazing."

That makes me feel a little more sure about it. The last thing I need on my conscience is Rowan being even harder on himself.

I sink onto the couch, leaving a good amount of distance between us. "If you thought that was good, wait until you experience the real thing."

He huffs and drops back into the couch. "At this rate, that will never happen."

"Not with that attitude it won't, soldier." I slap his thigh and stand up again. "I'll grab some chips and beer. No better way to follow up a jerking-off session than with alcohol, bad food, and an even shittier movie."

When I return, I set the bowl of chips and beer

bottles on the table and pick up the remote. I drop back into my spot, and Rowan uses that opportunity to shift closer. "This okay?" he asks.

"Yeah, man. Leon sits way closer than that."

And I didn't mean it as an invitation, but he takes it that way. Rowan moves onto the section of couch right next to mine, and when I sit back, our shoulders are almost touching.

Considering I *just* jerked off, there's no right to have this amount of sexual tension in the room. If he had an issue with a mutual stroke session, I can only imagine the complete freak-out he'd have if I straddled his lap and kissed him.

It's not something I should be thinking about anyway.

We already have a terrible history together, and he'll never be out if tonight is any indication. And while all this online attention has been amazing, I'm ready to find my forever person.

Fucking around with Rowan is a disaster waiting to happen.

And yet ... my dumb ass wants more.

I put an action movie on because I remember Rowan liking those, and it seems like the safest option. He sips his beer quietly, and I have no idea if he's actually paying attention to the movie or if his mind is doing what mine is. Straying back to an hour before, picturing him sprawled out on his bed naked, jerking himself until he came.

Damn, I bet it was a pretty sight.

Rowan looks up suddenly, catching me watching him. His blue eyes are muted by the color from the TV, but they still hold my stare in that captivating way they always have.

"Thank you," he says.

"What for?"

"Trying to help. I don't think anyone else has ever given enough of a shit to."

I tilt my head, not letting his words get to me. "Well, maybe if you'd let people in, they would have had that chance."

"Nah. No one wants to deal with a homophobic gay man. I can't imagine it's much fun for your partner to start crying and leave after sex."

Well, that's a fucking understatement.

Still, I can't let him know how awkward it was or make a big deal out of it.

"True, but it's the leaving part that's the issue. So next time, sob your heart out, then move on to something more fun. Like pizza. Or better still, round two."

He gives me a little shove, but he seems happier than before.

"Yeah? You find me a guy who'll let me sob all over them, and I might have to give it a try."

He turns back to the screen, and I watch the side of his face, trying not to concentrate on what he said.

The problem is, I've already found that guy.
I just wish he wasn't me.

FAKE FRIENDS

CHAPTER FOURTEEN
ROWAN

Waking up and finding Circus standing in his kitchen, wearing only a pair of sleep shorts, is too much for my tired gay brain. I want to touch him. I want to tell him how I can't stop thinking about him. I want to be the kind of guy who can offer him what he needs and prove to him that being with me is worth it.

To give him the big family he wants.

Pity none of that will happen.

I mumble out a good morning and then go in search of coffee. Morning me not think good. Need caffeine, stat.

Because at this point, I'm not convinced I'm done freaking out over last night.

I can probably count on two hands—maybe even one—the number of times I've had my dick sucked by a guy. And that's literally the entire range of my gay experience.

For a reason.

Every time I visited one of those clubs, hell, even the time with Circus, the high would last just long enough for me to drain my balls, and then the judgment would kick in. The massive crash of holy-shit-what-have-I-done takes over, and I run as fast and hard as I can.

Last night, there was no running.

Somehow Circus knew that what I needed wasn't space, it was to face him after what we'd done.

And now that's making me really uncomfortable. Because more than just getting off listening to the sound of his voice, last night felt ... right. We felt close.

Because Circus knows me the way literally no one else on earth does.

"What are your plans today?" he asks, and I can feel the way he's watching me. I'm not sure if he's waiting for the panic to kick back in, but I'm holding it together for now.

"Leita's having us over for lunch. They'll grill some burgers and try to set me up with whoever's currently single."

"Ouch."

He has no idea.

"Think you're up for a boyfriendly photo?"

Honestly? No. Just that word is kick-starting my heart into a rhythm it's not used to. But there's a deeper base need to get close to him that's difficult to ignore. Even as I tell myself it's wrong, even as I tell myself I'm being weak, I answer, "Sure."

Circus leads me over to the window overlooking the valley and wraps one arm around my front. He pulls me in until he's looking over my shoulder, out at the view. "Hug me like you mean it."

I have no idea what that looks like, but I close my eyes and wrap my arm around him tight. And there, tucked into my side, he feels like a gift. The voices quiet a little, and I use the brief reprieve to enjoy the feel of his body against mine.

"Perfect."

Circus tries to step away, but I don't let go. And when he turns his head to look up at me, it makes me smile to see his expression so unguarded.

"Come with me today?"

"What?" But he knows what I'm asking. His nervous laugh gives him away.

"To lunch. You used to eat at my place plenty growing up, so it's not like it will be weird. They'll just assume we're friends again. Then you can intercept all the women they're planning to throw my way."

"Like a reverse wingman?"

"Exactly." I squeeze my arm around him a bit tighter and let my other hand run over his back. My breathing won't work properly, but who needs oxygen at a time like this?

"I used to hate being at your place. Your family knew I wasn't straight, I could feel it."

"They didn't know anything."

He finally steps back out of my hold. "They knew. And they all *definitely* know now, because my dating history isn't a secret."

When he puts it like that ... just bringing him could

open up all those questions about my sexuality I've been actively avoiding for so long. I'll deny it, obviously, because having a queer friend doesn't automatically mean I'm gay. Especially since Circus and I go way back.

And maybe ... maybe having them start to ask the questions themselves might mean that if I ever do come out it won't be a total shock.

Then again, I'm not sure that will make much difference either way.

I wonder what it would be like to be openly gay. And have a supportive family. And to be able to wake up with a man in my bed and not have it trigger a panic attack.

"If it'd be too awkward for you, that's fine."

"Oh, it'll definitely be awkward. And not just for me, because if they ask, I'll tell them I've fucked men."

"To be fair, I don't think anyone's going to be asking you *that* question."

"Eh, seems likely."

My knee bounces. "So is that a yes?"

Instead of answering, Circus takes my hand and makes me follow him. It's not until we get to his bedroom door that I start to feel uneasy, and as he leads me to the bed, my whole brain is screaming *abort*.

I keep following.

Then Circus hands me a Magic 8-Ball. "Ask that. If it says yes, then I'll go."

"Is this a joke?"

"Nope. It's how I make all my important decisions."

I screw up my eyebrows as I eye him.

"For real. It's literally the reason you're here."

"And there was me thinking it had to do with my winning personality."

I give the ball a good shake, then hold my breath.

My sources say no.

Well, fuck. It was probably a stupid idea to begin with.

Circus covers the little window with his hand. "Maybe it only works for me." He takes the ball and gives it a good shake. "Should I go to the barbecue today?"

We wait.

Most likely.

"Well," he says. "That's good enough for me."

***

I love Sunbury and the sense of community it brings when everyone is together. For a family lunch, there are a lot of extra people here, and I'm undoubtedly happy I invited Circus to come with me.

Because as soon as I reach the backyard, Leita starts introducing me to all her single friends.

It's a game I know well. I've done the equivalent of

sneaking into Sunbury a few times over the past five years to attend birthday parties and holidays, and I'm always put on the same rotation.

Rowan, dance for the ladies.

I'm like a trained monkey.

But this time, Circus is there to field any questions that are too personal, by asking about their lives or turning it back on them. For someone people don't seem to know much about, he sure knows a lot about others.

By the time the next person arrives, they've forgotten all about me.

"Okay, it's official, you're my permanent reverse wingman for all of these events."

"Aww, but you didn't say please."

"Because I wasn't asking."

"Geez, one orgasm and he thinks he can control me."

My eyes fly wide, and I quickly look around to see if anyone's listening in.

"Relax, no one's around."

That assurance doesn't stop me from checking for myself. The last thing I need is to be outed at a party surrounded by family. I have a very real concern that if they ever find out, all I'm doing with Circus to stay in Sunbury will be for nothing.

Everything is linked to my family.

My friends, my job, where I live. I'm reliant on them in too many ways.

Levi goes darting past with one of the neighbors'

kids, and it makes me smile, the way they can be so involved in their little games and have no worries about the rest of us. I'll bet they have no idea what expectations are.

"You're thinking pretty hard over there."

I sigh. "I don't know how I'll ever willingly give all this up."

"Yeah," Circus says, voice more gravelly than usual. "It's pretty great. But ..."

"I know what you're going to say." Pointing out that conditional acceptance isn't what makes a family doesn't get me anywhere though.

He pins me with those deep gray eyes, and I can't look away. "I was going to say you have me now. And my friends. I know Tanner already likes you, and Royce barely likes anyone, but Jules and Mitch love *everyone*. Dahlia thinks you're hot"—he winks—"and Leon understands."

"Leon hates me." I laugh, thinking of the other night. "Actually, is he in love with you or something? Because he was giving off serious vibes."

Circus snorts. Loudly. "Definitely fucking not. I'm not his type, and he's not mine. Normally Leon doesn't give a shit what I do with my life, but he knows our history, and he saw the crush I had on you back then. He doesn't want me making the same mistakes."

Well, that's a relief. "I don't know." I shake my head. "They're your friends, Circus." I know them all because in

Sunbury you basically know everyone by extension, but since they were the year below me, we didn't cross paths much.

Whereas Circus and I were drawn to each other. I couldn't have escaped his pull if I tried. And it's happening again.

"All I'm saying is meet us at the bar tomorrow night. Hang out and relax. Be yourself. See two men being openly affectionate, and if you choose to let them know you're gay, none of them will say anything. We have each other's back always."

Inviting Circus to a family lunch. Hanging out with openly queer men who I *know* my family are leery of. It's like I'm determined to put a sign over my head saying *Gay as fuck*.

"Can I think about it?"

"Of course."

"Thanks."

Movement makes my gaze stray from Circus to my grandpa coming out of the house. He's carrying a salad that he plonks on the table, before heading in our direction.

I immediately stiffen. When he wears that pinched look, it's like I'm five years old again and he's just busted me wearing Mom's high heels.

"Rowan," he says, but he's staring hard at Circus. "And Kelly Atkins."

I jerk at the name, forgetting he always insisted on

calling Circus by his real name. Instead of getting pissed like when I did it, Circus slides his hands in the pockets of his floral-print shorts and rocks back on his heels.

"Old man Harvey."

"Listen, boy, we don't want any trouble."

Circus lets out a long breath. "Well, thank goodness for that. Trouble seems like way too much energy for this time in the day. If you'd requested it, I would have had to decline."

"I don't know what you're thinking, Rowan, bringing his kind around."

My throat feels thick and sticky, and I want to tell him to back off, but I can't.

"And what *kind* are you referring to?" Circus has lost the friendly tone now.

Grandpa bares his teeth like a dog exposing its hackles. "Homosexuals."

Circus gasps and pretends to look around. "There are *homosexuals* here?"

"Boy lovers." He's not bothering to keep his voice down now. "Like you."

"Oh, you've got it all wrong." At first, I actually think Circus is going to deny it. "I'm just a run-of-the-mill pansexual."

"Pan ... *what*?"

"It means I love cooking instruments. I just can't get enough."

Circus isn't keeping his voice down either, and I'm

torn in that place between laughing and crying, and I'm worried I might start to do both. At the same time.

"You brought him to a family event." Grandpa turns to me. "There are children here."

"Gramps, that's enough." Leita marches up to us, and she looks fierce. "This conversation is ending right now." She points a pair of salad tongs at Grandpa. "Go sit down and behave yourself, and stop making my guests uncomfortable. And you two, stop encouraging it. Other end of the yard, now."

"It's okay, Leita," Circus says. "I'm going to head off. Your grandpa says there's homosexuals around, and I wouldn't feel comfortable sharing food with one. They're not house-trained, you know."

"Don't be ridiculous," she snaps.

"I'll catch yas." He turns and heads for the house.

"No." The word leaves my mouth before I know what I'm saying. All I know is I want him here. Not as a wingman or a fake boyfriend. Just ... him. But I'm not Leita, and when I want to find my voice and speak out, it seems it's deserted me under the force of three stares. "I'll walk you out."

He looks disappointed, but it's nothing on how disgusted I am with myself.

And maybe it's the disgust that makes me say it, or something way deeper and *tired*, but as I pass Mom heading into the house, I turn to her and snap, "You couldn't do anything to shut him up?"

And look at me, throwing stones.

Because we're all just as spineless as each other.

"I'm so sorry," I finally say when we're alone.

"Yeah, I know." But he sounds bored, like it's too much of the same story for him.

I quickly glance over my shoulder and step closer. "I should have done better, I know that. But … I just couldn't make myself speak."

His fingers brush over mine, and he finally meets my eyes. "Come with me."

"Circus, I …" Want to. I want to so badly. Just leave the house and go hang out and deal with the consequences later. But I never could do it as a kid, and apparently, not much has changed. "I can't."

His fingers drop from mine, and he opens the door, walking out onto the porch. He looks back over his shoulder. "Last chance."

I don't say sorry, because it's not enough.

I close the door and return to the people who claim they love me.

But it couldn't be further from the truth.

FAKE FRIENDS

CHAPTER FIFTEEN
Circus

Maybe I should be mad about what went down at Leita's house, but any chance to make a homophobe look stupid is a fun time in my books.

It just sucks that Rowan couldn't join in. He didn't come for drinks on Sunday night either.

That visit, more than anything, reminded me that Rowan isn't in a place to start being open, but I really want to help him try.

Call it charity, call it human interest ...

The truth is, I want to see him naked again.

I shift uncomfortably as a niggling little voice tells me that's not *all* it is. Seeing him naked? Hell yes. But ... I can only imagine what it would be like to have to hide a massive part of myself, and it makes me sad. Having to deal with all that on your own would be lonely and isolating, and ... maybe I still care about him. A little.

I know all the reasons I shouldn't, but logic and emotion are refusing to mix.

Not to mention, with every day I get closer to my parents' anniversary, I'm starting to get more careless. In order to not *feel* how much I miss them, to not remind myself that this time five years ago they were helping me get through a broken nose, I shut it all down.

And I start to avoid Rowan too.

Because like it or not, he plays into a big part of their memory.

Besides, over the last few weeks, we've taken enough photos together to last me a while. I post a few times a day. Some with him and some without, and I haven't had to delete a photo in ages.

Progress.

Yet hanging over my head is the reminder we can't do this forever. The other couples are successful because they both post about each other. Sappy sweet stuff, sexy stuff, stuff that sells their love story and has people coming back for more.

At the moment, the mystery is all part of the fun. But there's an expiration date on people's patience, and if we "break up" without revealing who he is … what happens to me then? I was successful in my own right, but it's never been anything like this.

And there's still something about our photos that doesn't ring all the way true. No one else has picked up on it, but even though they're affectionate, they're missing that extra level.

I jump as my phone starts to vibrate in my hand and my manager's name appears on the screen.

"Good morning," he says in his sunny LA accent.

"This is early."

"I saw you post, so I knew you were awake. The boyfriend there?"

"Nope." I laugh. "You know the *friend* doesn't stay over."

"As long as no one else knows, we're doing okay."

I hum. Are we though? I'd be doing even better if I'd woken up next to him this morning. But I remind myself that's not going to happen.

Ever.

"Are you calling for a reason? Or just to check up on me?"

"Can't it be both?"

"Well, we've done the second one, let's move on to the point."

He chuckles, drawing out the suspense, which catches my interest. He normally launches straight into it, so this delay ...

"It's big, isn't it?"

"I may have had an interesting conversation this morning. For a fall/winter collection."

"With ..."

"Gucci Men."

I shoot to my feet. "There's no way."

"Then why am I looking at a proposed contract right now?"

"Have they seen my photos?" I start to laugh. "I'm not exactly high fashion."

"No, what you are is an insanely attractive man who

has gained a lot of clout in a very short amount of time. They want to capitalize on that. They want their brand to appeal to the next generation of men who are making a lot of money and choosing to spend none of it on clothes."

"People like that exist?"

"Have you met you?"

Shit. I pace to my window and look out at the valley. This is big. A Gucci campaign will gain a lot of social media attention, but there's also the old-school marketing as well. Billboards, buses and taxis, magazines.

It'll expand my reach way further than anything I'd ever accomplish on my own.

"What are the terms?"

He sighs. "Well, they originally asked for both of you, but I told them it wouldn't be possible, so we're currently renegotiating. They'll have to bring another model in for you to pose with, so you better make sure your guy is fine with that and that your followers know in advance. It's Gucci, so it's going to be high-end and a little sexy, but I've made it clear that there can't be any hints of anything romantic between you and whoever they choose. It's business only."

"Okay ..." I clear my throat. "But, if I could get both of us, they'd be interested?"

"They would, but they've made it clear there won't be any hiding his face."

"Not even a bit?"

"No. That was nonnegotiable. They've already got the shots they're using planned out, and they'll need you in LA for them."

Of course they do. They didn't get to be one of the biggest brands in the world by marketing on the fly.

"Should I ask him anyway?"

"There's no point now. They're already in the process of writing him out of the contract and looking for another model. How haven't you said yes yet? This is the biggest offer of your career so far."

That's the golden question, isn't it? *Why* haven't I said yes yet? A month ago, I would have been booking my flight already. "Send over the contract, and I'll let you know tomorrow."

"Circus—"

"That's my answer."

Preston doesn't say anything, but I can tell he's pissed. So I adopt the most bored tone I can manage because I know how it drives him crazy. "Anything else?"

"Eight a.m. That's as long as I'll give you."

"I'll talk to you tomorrow, then."

I hang up before he can push.

This could actually be the answer to how I maintain a brand without Rowan involved. If I do this, it'll lead to more followers, more interactions, which will lead to more opportunities.

Rowan and I could go our separate ways, and it

wouldn't impact on me *too* badly.

But ... I want to do this with *him*. I want us to go to Los Angeles and get lost in a world of hair and makeup and bright lights and people barking directions.

It'll be stressful and exhilarating, but will it be worth it if he's not there?

What am I doing?

Am I actually sitting here trying to justify talking myself out of an opportunity I've been working toward for years, just because some old flame is—barely—back in the picture?

Some old flame who *abandoned* me?

I try to draw up some of the old anger but come up empty.

Five years of holding on to the bitterness, and when I need it, it's nowhere to be found.

I guess Mom was right.

Once you forgive someone, you don't get to use it anymore.

So I do what I always do. I go to my bedroom, grab the 8-Ball, and let it make the choice for me.

"Should I ask Rowan?"

Without a doubt.

Looks like we're on the same page, then.

My determination to avoid him is forgotten as I get changed, grab my bike, and head into town. I probably could have called, but now I've thought about seeing him, I'm desperate to.

Who says people grow up?

Lucky for me, his car is in the diner parking lot, so he's clearly on the early shift. Piper is behind the counter when I walk in, so I assume Rowan must be out back.

"Well, this is a surprise," she says with a wide smile. "I swear I've never seen you in here so much in my life."

"Eh. You never had anything I wanted before. He through here?" I point to the door to the kitchen.

Piper eyes me for a moment. "We're starting our breakfast rush though, so if you go back there, you'll be helping."

As if I wasn't going to anyway.

I push through the door, and my smile is automatic when I see him leaning over the grill. He doesn't look up, so I go over to where the aprons are hanging on the wall and grab one.

"This a good look on me?"

Rowan jumps and almost drops his spatula on the hot surface. Oops. Probably shouldn't surprise a man while he's cooking. When he looks up, his smile is as automatic as mine was. "What are you doing here?"

"It's been a few days." Almost a week actually. "I wanted to stop by."

Yikes. And that's where I stop talking.

"You're out of photos, aren't you?"

"This is the first order?" I ask, pointing to a receipt

above the salad table.

"Yes ..."

I can feel his eyes on me as I grab a bun, break it in half, and slide it into the toaster.

"Press the green button," he says. "It's a timer."

I do, then finally turn to face him. "So I got an offer this morning."

"Oh yeah?" He scoops a fatty hunk of meat off the grill and onto a plate, next to a pile of scrambled eggs, then passes it through the return to Piper.

We're not exactly private here, so I'll have to watch my words.

"It was for a big brand. The shoot's in LA, and I can only imagine the kind of attention it'll bring me."

"That's awesome." He looks sincere. "Congratulations."

I don't respond. Instead, I turn my attention back to the burger bun as the timer sounds and check the receipt again. Relish, cheese, and onion. Rowan throws some eggs and bacon on the grill to finish it up.

"That's good, right?" he probes.

"Yes ... but I want to do it with you."

He almost drops the spatula again.

I laugh and grab his arm, pulling him away. "They asked for both of us. The shoot will be super high-end and tasteful, but there'll definitely be a sexual element involved. So I totally get it if you're not interested."

"Circus ..."

I consider telling him that they only want both of us. That without him, I can't do it. Because I know how good he'll be, but I also can't put that kind of pressure on him. "Look, just think about it today. No one around here pays attention to brand names, but the shots *will* be in magazines and online, so there's a higher chance someone will see them. That said, it's *just* modeling. It means nothing. And it's a lot of money." I glance around the kitchen. "That fifty K is small-fry compared to what they're offering. Two hundred K. You could get out of here, do whatever the hell you want."

Rowan catches me completely by surprise when he steps forward and covers my mouth with his hand. There's a tiny smile on his lips as he looks down at me, and I swear my heart kicks up a notch. "You want me to do it though?"

I nod.

He takes a minute to study me. "Let me think about it. And in the meantime …" He waves a hand to the receipts. "Your orders are banking up."

I laugh. "Oh no, I was just helping until the conversation was over. Which it is now, so …"

"I'm thinking about helping you with your career, you can help out here in return. And who knows, maybe if you're *really* good at it, I might even say yes."

I hold back my groan in favor of a smile and grab the next receipt. "One fried embryo and some pig flesh thanks."

He laughs. "I don't think breakfast has ever sounded so classy."

CHAPTER SIXTEEN
ROWAN

I get to the Ugly Mug early so I can polish off a beer before anyone else arrives. Having drinks with Circus's friends is intimidating, but since this is the second time he's invited me, I guess I should probably show.

His request from this morning won't stop running through my mind.

Neither will the way he looked in that apron, though that's for *other* reasons. Who knew domesticity could be so hot?

I'm glad Mom and Dad weren't in to witness it though, because they would have lost their shit about him being back there. Insurances and whatever. Plus, you know, after what happened at Leita's, he's not exactly their favorite person.

I'm glad he broke and came to see me, because I was one shift away from driving out to his house and apologizing again. I get the feeling he doesn't like when I do that.

Reynolds slides my drink across the counter, and I thank him before he moves away.

I wasn't lying when I said I'd think about the offer.

The money's a lot. And *a lot* would be a huge help toward doing something of my own around here.

I slide my phone out of my pocket and open the account of the influencers Circus showed me the other week. I'm not going to lie, I like looking at them. They're both really hot and have their own accounts, but while Circus might not know if they're dating or not, I'm convinced. The way they talk about each other, so openly, is what keeps me coming back to them.

The whole mystery of *him* is great, but already people are asking when they're going to see my face and whether I'm actually ugly as fuck, and I get the feeling that as fun as this is, it's not going to last.

They want to know who I am.

And that's terrifying.

It doesn't stop a tiny piece of me from being curious though.

If I were to start my own account, and *if* I were to start showing my face and letting people in, there has to be a way to block people, right? If I could find out the accounts of people in town, all I'd have to do is make sure they didn't have access to see my stuff. It'd be a lot of work, but ... it's doable. Surely.

It wouldn't stop people without an account from finding me, but those people would have to know what they're looking for first.

And if I did that and set up certain sponsors the way Circus has, when this whole thing ends I might still be able to keep making money that way.

At least short term.

It's not something I could imagine sustaining my life, because I want a job that's active. But it could complement it, right?

Holy shit. I'm actually trying to talk myself into this.

I've known for a while that I want more than anything to be living life as an openly gay man, but I've had no idea how to even make that happen without massive repercussions. Seeing the way Circus's followers have supported us right from the start though, posting those photos and pretending they're real, even the accidental phone sex, has me craving that life more than ever. And I'm starting to wonder if there's a way for me to have it all.

An openly gay man online, maybe a male *roommate*, and nothing has to change as far as my family is concerned.

Too bad my head is still holding me back.

"Rowan, hey!" Tanner calls out to me from a booth he and Royce have just sat down in. I drain the rest of my beer and order another three before joining them.

"Cheers," Royce says as I slide his over. We've never spoken much, but Tanner's mom and mine used to run the church bake sales together.

"How've you been?" Tanner asks, and Royce snorts out a laugh.

I glance at him. "What?"

"Don't mind Tanner. He's just been drooling over your tattoos since you got back."

Tanner starts to splutter and turns a dark shade of red. "Not ... drooling ..."

"Apparently he likes bad boys."

Which is hilarious because Royce is the furthest thing from a bad boy I've ever seen. He has shiny brown hair, a baby face, and more freckles than skin. He's also way skinnier than Tanner which makes them look like a weird pair next to each other.

"I hate to break it to you, Tanner, but I'm basically a saint."

I slide into the booth with them, and the knot of anxiety in my gut eases up a bit.

Until a familiar, sexy laugh sounds from behind me. "'Saint?' Clearly I need to work on my corruption skills."

I'm down for it, I want to say but can't. Circus would call me on it anyway.

He slides into the spot next to me and steals a sip of my beer before placing it back in front of me.

I can't say I hate the familiarity of the action, even if I do glance around to see who's in here. Friday nights don't usually get busy until later though, and no one is paying attention to our table.

It helps me to relax.

I grin at Circus, and he grins right back.

"Who else is coming?" Tanner asks. Royce is sipping his beer, looking back and forth between us.

"Leon and Dahlia."

"No Jules tonight?"

"Nah, she's not feeling well."

I sort of wish *Leon* wasn't feeling well so I didn't have to face him, but I guess I need to get it done sooner or later.

But when he shows up with Dahlia, he says hey and that's it. No teasing or ribbing or hinting at the shit he knows about me. Progress?

Circus leaves to buy a round and comes back with food as well. And even if I don't particularly fit in here, it's nice to be surrounded by conversation that doesn't have any weight to it. Leon talks about work and his latest *male* hookup, and I hang on to every word. Dahlia's teaching at the high school we used to attend, and Royce and Tanner are in the process of finalizing the sale on their house and their plans for once they have.

And those two are so affectionate with each other, I can't stop looking at them.

Circus leans in and his lips brush my ear. "You're staring."

"Can you blame me?"

When I turn so I can see his face, his expression is soft. "Is there anything wrong with *them*?" he whispers, tilting his head in their direction.

"Well, no, of course n—"

"Then why would there be something wrong with you?"

"It's not ..." I clear my throat and look around to make sure no one is listening in. Leon seems like he might be, and Royce is watching us, but I *think* he's too far away to hear anything. "It's just hard."

"I know." His hand finds mine under the table, and I suck in a sharp breath. "No one is saying you need to jump in and throw your own pride parade. I'm only saying, baby steps. Do little things each day that can get you to that point. Whether it's telling that stupid voice to fuck off—or your grandpa, but make sure I'm there for that—or, I don't know ..."

This time I duck my mouth to his ear. "Or watch gay porn?"

He swallows. "Or that."

"I have been, you know. I never used to be able to shut off my thoughts, but I've been trying. And that negative voice has been overridden with a new one."

"Oh, yeah?"

"Yeah. And the new voice sounds scarily like someone I know."

"Hmm. Sounds hot."

"You have no idea." My voice dips, snagging his attention, and the energy that burns between us makes me wish I could follow through.

"You guys fucking?"

I jump at the question, and everyone turns to look at Royce.

"W-what?"

Circus laughs. "If we were fucking, do you really think I'd keep it to myself? *Look* at the man."

"A month ago you couldn't stand the sight of him, and now you guys are looking at each other like crack."

"They are?" Tanner's eyebrows wrinkle up.

"Isn't Rowan straight?" Dahlia asks.

"Don't you know better than to assume?" Royce asks, hooking a thumb at Tanner. Tanner grabs his hand and bites his thumb, distracting people from the question for approximately a second before they turn to me.

My throat feels hot.

"That's a dumb question," Circus says. "Assume away."

It doesn't distract anyone. "Wait, are you not?" Dahlia pushes.

"Hey, look a bird in the bar!" Circus continues. "Everyone turn and look at the invisible bird that's flying around just over—"

I cover his mouth with my hand again. Because I can. Because I sort of love it.

"Ah …" I glance around at them all. Can I trust them with this? I know Circus said I could, but if just one person lets it slip, even by accident …

But Circus and Leon already know and haven't said anything.

Tanner and Royce surely would know outing someone isn't okay.

I eye Dahlia. "Would it matter if I wasn't straight?"

She picks up her beer and glances inside. "Is there something in the water? Why are *all* the guys here gay?"

Tanner lifts a hand. "Bi."

"Pan," Circus adds.

She sighs. "Shut up. You know what I mean."

I swallow roughly and lift my hand. It's shaking. I can't believe I'm about to say this. I quickly look around, and when I'm sure it's all clear, I say, "Gay." Only it gets caught in my throat, and I'm not sure if they even understand the word. I lock eyes with Leon, who gives me a small smile.

"And if that's repeated outside of this group," Leon says, "your lives will be made miserable."

My jaw wants to drop, but I hold it together.

I quickly hide my shaking hands in my lap, getting increasingly worried I'm going to start crying. Which I will not do. Not here.

Not even when Circus grabs my hand under the table and gives it a tight squeeze.

Then doesn't let go.

Not even when the conversation continues on and no one makes a big deal out of my declaration.

Not even when Tanner jokingly tells Royce that he wants in on a Row and Roo sandwich.

Or when Roo's face goes completely blank and he says to me, "I will gut you."

It's all ... so normal.

And ... I'm *out*. To a handful of people, but it still

counts.

I feel sick.

And excited.

And like moving from this booth will be too big to manage.

I'm also borderline ready to take it all back and disappear from town again, but I firmly push that thought aside. And the voice that sounds like Circus reminds me this is okay.

No one is judging me.

Except for myself, and that's something I *can* change.

By the time I get home that night, I'm more excited than scared.

Way too excited to sleep.

So instead, I sit down, grab my laptop, and start searching. I open an account, then hunt down every social media account of anyone in town who could potentially find the photos of Circus and me.

Block, block, fucking *block*, motherfuckers.

By the time I'm done, my eyes are scratchy, my neck is sore, and I've blocked a few *thousand* people. It's almost morning and thank God I'm not working today because my only plan is to sleep.

But before I can lose the nerve, I add a display picture, then find a photo of Circus and me from high school. It's faded slightly, and I have to take a photo of it before I can upload it, but it's of us at our spot on Crown

Trails. Circus is leaning back into my chest, both of us wearing huge smiles as the sun beats down on our faces.

I clear my throat and type out a caption.

Thank God for your smiles.

And I mean it.

Then I tag him and hover over the *About Me* option on my profile. My brain is too tired to think, so all I type is one word.

Him.

Then I fall face-first into bed and pass out.

CHAPTER SEVENTEEN
CIRCUS

I can't believe my eyes.

When I was talking baby steps, I never for a second thought Rowan would come out to a group of people and then claim me online.

But there it is.

Him.

And there's a clear shot of his face and a photo of us from years ago. I didn't have my septum or ear pierced then, and Rowan had none of his tats. But they're in his display picture, and it hasn't taken long for people to work out what's going on here.

I hope he locked down his personal accounts, because the fan hordes are coming for him.

It's insane. He's gained tens of thousands of followers overnight, and the number keeps ticking higher. People are asking for more photos, more details, *more.*

Holy shit it's him
Huh, he's not an ugly POS
Fuck, damn. I'm available. Here's my number ...
I'd ride him like a horse.

IT'S H!M OH MY GOD IT'S HIM srghaer;gh!!

I can only imagine what his notifications look like this morning because mine are probably the same.

This is a great way to get noticed. Photographers, designers, maybe even movie producers ...

But I can't get hold of Rowan all morning. Preston is blowing up my phone with calls and messages, pressuring me for an answer on this shoot, but I don't know how I want to play this.

Was the account Rowan's way of letting me know he's in? Or was he drunk, and is he going to regret this the second he wakes up?

It's already after midday and he's still MIA.

My mind starts turning the dramatics up a notch as I picture his family seeing this, and suddenly I'm worried.

Have they seen it? Oh fuck, what if they've kicked him out? And he doesn't have his phone?

I grab my shit and leave.

Taking the car is faster than my bike, and it doesn't take long before I'm pulling up in front of his place.

From what I can tell, it doesn't *look* like there's been any fighting or destruction, but then again, kicking the shit out of someone's house isn't how we do confrontation in Sunbury.

I gather my nerves and approach the front door, praying Grandpa Dickwad isn't the one who answers.

Luck must be on my side, because it's his mom instead.

Which, you know, is only fractionally better, but I'll take it.

"Circus?"

"Morning. Rowan home?" I resist crossing my fingers and focus on sending good vibes her way.

"I think he's still in his room ..."

That sounds like an invitation to me. I pull open the screen door and step past her. "Thanks. I remember where that is."

Then I hightail it up there before she can think to try and stop me.

As I walk down the hall, I'm hit with that awkward moment of déjà vu. A thousand memories of walking this exact same path come at me, and instead of anger or sadness, all I feel is lingering regret that we didn't make the most of our time together.

I knock lightly on Rowan's door, and when there's no answer, I crack it open and slip inside.

He's still out cold. And given how no one has stormed down the hall to kick me out, I'd say the account hasn't been discovered yet.

The ball of worry unravels as I look at his peaceful form. He's under the covers, so I can't make out much of anything except his bare shoulders and the tops of his arms that are buried under his pillow.

I creep closer to the bed and run my hand over his back. "Wake up, sleepyhead."

He jerks up and takes a moment to blink the room

into focus. "What's going on?"

"Just your friendly neighborhood wake-up call."

"Circus ..." He looks around as though confirming he's in *his* bedroom.

"Can confirm, I have not kidnapped you."

He smiles sleepily before flopping back down on his pillows. The blanket has moved down farther, revealing his smooth, toned back. He pats the mattress beside him, and unlike his mom, *that* was an actual invitation.

Don't mind if I do.

"What's going on?" he asks sleepily.

I reach over to smooth out the bird's nest his hair has become. "You tell me, Mr. I'm-going-to-broadcast-my-closeted-ass-online."

"Argh." That wakes him up. He plucks my phone from my hand, punches in my passcode—and okay, *when* did he work that out?—and opens the app. "I really did it?"

"You really did."

He taps on the photo he posted last night, and it takes him through to his account. "*How* many followers?"

I start to laugh. "Welcome to crazy town."

"Wow." He drags his hand back through his hair, ruining the progress I'd made on taming it. "Okay, so that wasn't a dream at all."

"You all right?" I ask cautiously.

"Yeah ... I am."

"What if someone sees this?"

He shakes his head. "I blocked everyone I could find."

"And if you missed someone?"

"I guess I'll deal with that if it happens." He hands me back my phone. "Here, take a photo." Rowan rolls back onto his stomach and loops an arm around my waist before pressing his face into my side.

My heart thumps harder as I mess up my hair and settle in, like I've just woken up too. I aim for a sleepy smile, and when I take the photo and check the picture, I almost don't want to post it. Because it feels too personal. And it's a lie.

Rowan takes my phone again, and when he sits up, his shoulder presses against mine. "What do we type?"

"Ooh, go super corny. 'He's my dream' type bullshit."

Rowan laughs and types it out then posts it. "This is actually kind of fun."

"Because I'm a fun kind of guy."

"No arguing there."

"So ..." I tease, reaching over him for *his* phone. "Gay porn you say?"

"Oh, fuck."

"You're going to have to unlock your phone, because unlike you, I have boundaries."

"Which is why you helped yourself to every one of my drinks last night?"

"Ah, porn. Back to that."

He chuckles and holds up the phone so it can scan his face.

I settle back into the bedframe and start my search. "Let's see what's in your history ..."

"It's cute you think I wouldn't have deleted it immediately."

I tap over to the private browser.

"Deleted from there too," he points out unnecessarily.

I pout. "You're no fun. I only want to know what kind of freaky stuff you're into."

"How horrible of me not to enlighten you."

He's clearly not going to change his mind. Fine, then. I hand the phone back as mine starts to vibrate again. I hesitate at Preston's name.

"So ... remember that Gucci offer I told you about yesterday?"

"Sure do."

"I was supposed to get back to them this morning."

"Ah, shit. Sorry."

"All good. But ... is it a yes? I mean, you set up your own account and ..."

His blue eyes narrow as he stares at the opposite wall, clearly turning it all over in his head. "Okay. Let's do it."

"Even though there'll be no hiding?"

He cringes. "Feeling less confident, but sure."

"Yes!" I could kiss him I'm so excited. But the last thing I want is to create any freak-outs, so I grab my phone and busy my hands instead.

Me: *We're both in.*

The reply comes quicker than expected.

Preston: *I know you didn't just say 'we' when I was very clear that your boy wasn't involved*

Me: *New number, who dis?*

Preston: *You're going to be the death of me. I swear to fucking God, Circus …*

FAKE FRIENDS

CHAPTER EIGHTEEN
ROWAN

I guess I know how Batman feels.

Leading a secret life is exciting as balls, and with every day getting us closer to our LA trip, I'm getting pumped.

The whole social media thing isn't a huge buzz for me the way it is for Circus, but I'm starting to understand why that is. The influx of messages and comments are super positive—it's like having an extended family.

That would be pretty hard to resist for someone with no family at all.

It's beginning to feel like, more than ever, I'm being torn in two directions.

The person I *am* posts photos and has fun with Circus and goes out to drinks with his friends. Tanner and Royce got the keys to their house, so I've stopped around to help them with some demolition, and Leon even talks to me when he comes into the diner for coffee before starting his long days.

The person I'm *supposed* to be works at the diner and helps Grandma in the kitchen and watches football with Grandpa. I keep my mouth shut and my head down, and try to ignore that voice that keeps telling me I'm being deceitful to everyone.

Well, everyone except Circus.

He's the only one who actually knows what I'm going through and is there for me anyway. And even though I shouldn't, even though I have next to nothing to offer him, I'm falling for him all over again.

Except this time, it's not some high school fascination. It's not awe or idolization. I look at him and feel warm inside. I look at him and can imagine coming out and telling people who I am and not hiding anymore.

But then the voice reminds me it's impossible.

I sit with my family during Sunday mass, letting my thoughts drift back to the day before. Circus drove us out to a water hole that I didn't know existed. It was in the middle of the forest and looked like someone had cut a perfect hole into the ground and filled it with crystal clear water. We spent hours just goofing off and hanging out before he even remembered we were supposed to be taking photos. It was nice. It gave me just a little insight into how having a boyfriend might be.

Well, sort of. I can't imagine anyone coming close to matching Circus.

His friend Jules starts to play a hymn on the piano at the front of the church, and the people around me start to sing. I don't join in, even though I know every word, because how can I sing about a great and powerful God who loves everyone, when in the priest's next breath, he makes it clear God doesn't love *me*?

I refuse to believe it though. I might have struggled with my sexuality, but I've never struggled with my faith. Because when I imagine God, I imagine a different entity to the one the churches force on me.

I look around the room, noting the lack of familiar faces. No Circus—he told me he stopped coming after his parents died—no Tanner and Royce or Dahlia or Leon. Jules's boyfriend is down the front along with Rafe and Laura, who Circus used to hang out with in school.

And if Tanner and Royce and Leon can fall in love with men and not attend church, yet all be leading happy, healthy lives ... Why can't I?

Why *can't* I?

A weight transfers off my shoulders and sinks into my gut as I stand up midsong ...

Ignore the confused glances ...

And walk out.

***

I head to the diner and open up early. My family is already going to be angry that I walked out on Sunday mass, so this can be my penance.

No sooner have I unlocked the doors—a whole hour early—than Leon sticks his head inside.

"I thought you guys were closed Sunday morning?"

"Usually are."

He pushes inside and pulls up a stool at the counter. His eyes have dark smudges underneath them, and his graying hair is a mess.

"Long night?" I can barely make out his grin behind his beard.

"Oh yeah. I have a few bruises to prove it."

"Say what now?"

He laughs and glances around. "Once you go gay, you'll understand."

"At this stage that feels like it will never happen."

"That's too bad. If I had to miss out on sex, I'd go nuts."

"I'm already halfway there."

"Not surprised." He watches me. "Especially with all those photos you've been taking with Circus. I'd find it impossible to keep my hands to myself after taking hot photos with the guy I'm into."

"What makes you think I'm into him?"

Leon laughs. "You two are like magnets. No point trying to deny it, I'm not an idiot. Can you put a black coffee on for me, please? I haven't had a minute's sleep, and I need to head over to Port Welling before starting work on my place."

I start his coffee. "Are you doing up your house as well?"

"I am. There's a lot of old houses around here that need a bit of loving."

"That's true. My grandparents' place was getting old

by the time we moved them out of there."

"Well, now's a good time to buy if you're sticking around. There have been a few people driving up on the weekends, looking at land. The bigger Portland gets, the more it pushes people out. And Sunbury is a good distance for a quiet life but big-city money. Plus once the shopping complex I've been contracted for gets built over at Port Welling, there'll be even more people sniffing around."

I hand Leon his coffee. "Yeah, but it'll mean we need more businesses around here to make the place more attractive."

He grunts and takes a sip of the steaming drink. "Like a gym. It's a pain in the ass driving over to Port Welling every time I want to work out."

"A gym." I rub my chin. "You think there's enough interest for that?"

"I think people around here would kill for it."

Well, Leita and her mom's group are always heading over to Port Welling too. It sets the gears in my head in motion.

"I have to admit, I've missed working out too. And I've been looking for a way to get out of this diner ... maybe *I* should open a gym?"

Surprise flickers across his features. "That would mean ... you're sticking around?"

"Yeah. Circus and I made a deal that if I help out and play fake boyfriend, Circus forgets about trying to get me to leave."

"Interesting." Leon doesn't look happy.

"What's that face for?"

"Real talk. I told Circus I would back off you and let him do whatever he needed to because you were leaving. If you guys needed to fuck and move on, then fine. But I knew that sooner or later, you'd be out of town."

My brain is still stuck on *fuck*. I shake my head. "Remind me what any of that has to do with you?"

"Circus is my best friend, and I don't want to see him get hurt again. You have no idea what it was like after ... you know. Even after what you did, he wouldn't say a bad word about you. He refused to report it and told me I didn't understand. I know *now* what he was talking about with the whole homophobic family thing, but that still doesn't make it okay."

"*I* know that. And like I told him, I'll probably never forgive myself. But that doesn't mean I need you throwing it back in my face every time I see you."

"And I'm not trying to." He sets his cup down. "I want him to be happy. If you can do that, fine, stick around, date, whatever you need to do. But if you can't make him happy—and if you're never planning to come out, that would be a no—you've got to tell him that. Leave him alone, stop playing happy families, and both of you can move on."

I know Leon is talking sense and that he has Circus's best interests in mind. I know he's looking out for his friend and this is him being kind and whatever else, but ...

"I'm not saying this to be a dick, but you have to let me work that out in my own time."

"But—"

"Nope. Sorry, Leon. I know what you're saying and why, but at the end of the day, people don't go out of their way to hurt the people they care about. And I care about him a lot. I'll never, *ever* hurt him physically again, there's no doubt there, but when it comes to anything else ..." I wipe over the grinds I left on the counter after making his coffee, trying to sort through what I'm saying. "It's complicated. I know what I *want*, but it's so hard to let myself go for it when I'm constantly second-guessing everything."

He looks awkward as he spins his saucer around once, twice, before looking up at me. "You care about him?"

"God, Leon. So much."

"Do you know what today is?"

FAKE FRIENDS

CHAPTER NINETEEN
Circus

Fuck. Today.

I stare at a random spot on the floor, slumped down in my couch and wishing the world would go and fuck itself with a giant barbed dildo.

Five years today since I last saw their faces.

Since I saw the fierce flash in Mom's eyes every time she caught sight of my broken nose.

Since Dad smiled warmly as he brought me soup for lunch.

They were never supposed to go out that night.

They were supposed to help me get over my heartbreak, and see me graduate, and send me off to college.

I take another sip of the scotch and hold back my gag.

I hate scotch.

But it was Dad's favorite, so it seems fitting.

To sit and get wasted.

To watch the day pass outside, while I sit here, completely forgotten about.

Leon will be over at some point to make sure I

haven't killed myself, but the joke's on him because I'm not suicidal.

Or is it on me?

Because maybe if I was, the pain would go away.

Instead, all I have left of them is a deep ache behind my sternum that's infecting my bloodstream.

And it *hurts*.

It hurts to know this was never supposed to be my life.

I was meant to study business and become a suit. To visit home on the weekends and call my parents every night.

Maybe I even would have taken them for granted and forgotten to check in while I was at college having my first adult experiences.

I'll never know.

All I know is that I won't be visiting them at home or forgetting about them, ever.

And to really drive the point home, it's Mother's Day next week. Thank fuck I'll be in LA.

I sigh heavily and it seems too loud in the quiet, empty house.

Maybe I shouldn't have sold my childhood home. Would I have ever gone back there? My sources say fucking no.

But my dumbass seventeen-year-old self took that option away.

I frown as I register a tapping noise, but it goes

away.

I lift the bottle of scotch to my lips and this time take an even longer drink.

I'm tempted to grab my phone and check my notifications. Check and make sure people still love me and remind myself there are people in the world thinking of me in this exact moment, but my phone is locked away.

Because I know too well that getting blind drunk and social media do not mix.

I blink and sit up a little, sure I heard a creak. The noise is gone now, but *did* I? Or is it just the alcohol messing with my head?

"Want company?"

I jump about a foot and spin to see Rowan standing in the doorway. "You trying to give me a heart attack?"

He doesn't answer. I take another drink. Then burp loudly.

"Hells no to company. Today's my day to get wasted, and I'm not having anyone around to judge me for it."

He walks closer anyway. "You've never judged me for my shit," he says as he reaches out and pries the bottle from my hand. "And I'll never judge you for yours. Besides, that would be pretty hypocritical of me when I'm planning on getting blackout drunk too."

"What?"

"Misery loves company, right?" He takes a long drink, then shudders as it goes down. "Bottoms up."

"You know …" I stand, stepping forward until I'm well within his personal space. "When a gay man says that, it has an entirely different meaning."

I take the bottle and as I drink, I watch his Adam's apple bob up and down as he swallows thickly.

"Good to know," he says.

"Mmhmm. And I'd be more than happy to do as I'm told."

Rowan starts to laugh, but I pick up on the way it's slightly off-key. I've rattled him. Which is perfect. Having the alcohol swimming through my veins makes it way easier to say what I've been thinking for weeks, and he better hurry up and catch up to my level of intoxication, or he's not going to be drunk enough to handle me.

He takes my arms and steers me back toward the couch.

I fall backward and a bit of scotch sloshes out of the bottle and over my hand. Rowan takes it from me as he sits too, so I turn, catch his eyes, then very slowly start to drag my tongue through the alcohol on my fingers.

His groan sends waves of pleasure across my skin. "No more of that."

"Of what?"

He narrows his eyes. "You're teasing me."

"Fucking duh." I flatten out my tongue and drag it from my wrist, up over my palm.

"Circus …" His voice is husky, and I love the sound.

"If you're determined to stay …" I wriggle closer and

steer the bottle back to his lips. "Drink up, boyfriend."

He only hesitates a second before he does what I say. "So, is this what you've been doing all day? Or do you go visit them too?"

I snort. "Nope, I just drink. I, umm ..." I turn away from him and take another sip from the bottle. "I haven't actually been to their graves. Other than the funeral."

"What?"

His disbelief puts me on the defensive. "Why the hell would I want to? Like, wow, what an amazing way to remind myself that my only family are dead."

"Sorry ..." he whispers.

The scotch is buzzing in my veins. "I don't want to talk about them."

"Okay."

"Okay."

Silence falls between us for a while, Rowan clearly as lost in thought as I am. "I walked out of church this morning."

The weight of that slides through my drunken haze. "No way, really?"

"Yep. Wasn't subtle about it either. Halfway through and I was like, fuck this, and left."

"I'm impressed."

"Thanks. And now I'm hiding out here so I don't have to face what my family is going to say about it."

"Aren't we a pair?" I ask as he passes the bottle back to me. "We both have family issues. You have too much, and I have none at all. Could you imagine being part of one of those well rounded, healthy family dynamics?"

"Do they exist?"

"The TV says yes."

His tone turns mocking. "And do we believe everything we see on TV, Circus?"

"Always."

"Zombies?"

"Totally real."

"*Umbrella Academy*?"

"Documentary, right?"

He laughs. I'm addicted. "Explain Elmo to me."

"What's to explain? He's cuddly and red."

"But why does he laugh so much?"

"Because he's ticklish, duh." It gives me an idea. "What about you?"

I wriggle my fingers into his ribs, and he lets out the most adorable laugh as he squirms to get away from me. "Enough, I concede."

The last thing I want to do is stop, but I remind myself of a thing called self-control which is becoming more and more distant as the drinking goes on. We pass the bottle between us, as we talk about the most stupid things, and every time one of us comes close to talking about our families and bringing down the mood, we wingman each other out of there.

All I wanted when today started was to drink and cry, but Rowan has eased some of that all-consuming pain, and the more time I spend with him, the more relaxed I am.

Well, the more time I spend with him *and* the scotch.

Because *damn* I'm buzzed.

"My fingers are all tingly," I tell him.

He takes one hand and starts to kiss each fingertip. "How do you feel now?"

Am I drooling? "Tingly, but for another reason."

He smirks and flicks his tongue over one of them. "And now?"

My groan gets stuck in my throat, and before I can answer, he sucks my finger into his mouth.

"Erect," I gasp. "Definitely feeling erect."

He lets my hand drop like dead weight into my lap. Rowan presses his lips to my ear. "I was pretending that was your dick."

A shiver racks my body. "Why are you getting me excited over nothing?"

"Isn't that what your bottoms up comment was?"

"The difference is, I'm perfectly prepared to follow through."

"Really…" He shifts closer, sliding his legs underneath mine. "Tell me what you'd have me do to you."

"Are you sure your poor closeted dick could handle it?"

"He'll behave. Someone taught me the importance of

jerking off before I come here." His breath is heavy with the taste of scotch, and I know mine isn't any better. We're both half-wasted which is the only reason we're even having this conversation in the first place. Which leads me to the question: Why haven't we gotten drunk together before now?

"I could make you *come* here."

"I have exactly zero doubts about that." His voice is deep, and despite what he said about jerking off, I'd bet my house he's as turned on as I am right now. My restraint is stretched thin, and I'm just waiting for one of us to snap.

"Want to know how?"

"Yes. Always yes."

I lean into him, and his arms automatically close around me. "First, I'd strip you naked, exposing every one of those muscles that drive me crazy. Then I'd kiss you. Slow at first, then deeper and harder until I had to stop so you could catch your breath."

His hands tighten on me, and I feel them start to shake. "Would you be naked too?"

"Only if you did it. Only if you popped each button open, until you could touch every inch of skin you wanted. Then you'd slide my pants over my hips and see exactly how hard I am for you."

"Fuck." Rowan's head drops back, so I lean forward and lick a stripe up his neck. He tastes like salt and man, and a moan leaves me as I pant against his skin.

I need to pull back. End this.

I know if I keep pushing, I'll take things too far.

But then Rowan whispers into my ear, "What else?"

"I know you remember how good my mouth is. And trust me when I say it's gotten even better. Your dick, your balls ..." I pause before taking it one bit further. "Your hole."

Rowan jerks back and I'm worried for a second that this is the too-far point, but then I see his face. His eyes are wide, his breathing is shallow and erratic.

He starts to lean forward, so slowly I swear he's fighting himself on it. I'm holding my breath to see what will happen.

And then his lips brush over mine.

His hands shake as he cups my face, but they don't seem as bad as usual. I can feel the way he's holding himself back though. Restraining. Attempting to hold on to a quivering semblance of control.

I close my eyes and memorize the feel of him. His lips, his scent, his strong hands.

He pulls back, nose brushing mine, and our eyes clash.

A second stretches between us. Then two.

He moves before I can prepare myself.

Rowan tackles me back into the couch, and his mouth crashes into mine. It's hard and demanding, and as soon as he works my lips open, his tongue surges into my mouth. I feel his groan right down to my toes.

His kisses are desperate, and I respond with as much passion, and it's just now occurring to me how starved for affection I am. I can only imagine how it must be for him.

To never let himself touch or look or give in to these feelings, and all that pent-up need is coming through loud and clear.

"Kelly," he pants into my mouth.

The sound of my name sets me on fire. I part my legs and pull him flush against me, and the feel of his heavy body on mine, his hard cock rutting against my own, makes my brain check out.

I can't focus. Can't think. All I can do is feel and kiss and grind against him.

His groan echoes mine, and his breathing picks up a notch. I bend my knees more and grab his ass, encouraging every thrust that works deeper, harder. My shorts are painful against my throbbing cock, but Rowan seems to have lost all control.

He starts to grunt as he picks up the pace, and then his whole body goes stiff.

His moan is long and drawn-out, and he collapses on top of me, kisses turning slower and more sensual.

Meanwhile I've still got a raging hard-on.

"Come with me." I ease up and grab his hand, dragging him with me to my bedroom. My thoughts are cloudy with lust as I push him back on the bed and slowly strip out of my clothes. Then I reach down and start to stroke myself.

His eyes zero in on the sight.

Rowan's mouth falls slack as I start to jerk myself faster, working myself back to orgasm.

"Can I?" he whispers.

I step forward and he immediately scrambles to the edge of the bed. When his hand closes around the taut skin of my cock, my knees almost buckle.

"Oh God, yes. Please."

He gives a long, slow pump, and I want to cry.

"Faster."

I don't need to tell him twice. Rowan picks up the pace, and his big hand doesn't take long to get me to the edge.

I don't have a chance to warn him.

Tingles race from the base of my spine to my balls as my orgasm explodes. My eyes slam closed as I drop my head back, letting the waves roll over me. It subsides as I concentrate on evening out my breathing.

Only then do I look at him.

Hair a mess, lips red and wet and swollen. Blue eyes still as hazy with alcohol as my brain feels, which can be the only reason he hasn't freaked out yet.

I've come over the front of his shirt, and a small amount has hit his chin. I duck down and with one lick, I gather it on my tongue, grab his hair to tilt his head back, and kiss him.

He gasps into my mouth but kisses me just as

passionately as before.

When we finally break apart, we're both panting.

"I'll get you some clothes."

"Yeah ... thanks."

I'm worried that voice in his head is trying to come back. "And the scotch?"

"Definitely the scotch." He stands and starts to strip off.

I know I'm supposed to be doing something, but my brain is all, *What clothes?* and chooses to gape at him instead.

When he removes his shorts to reveal his cock hanging heavy and thick between his legs, mine perks up, ready for round two.

I force my attention away and dress the man.

But he only pulls on the underwear I hand him and then settles under the covers.

Well, when in Rome. I pull on some underwear too, grab the scotch, and climb in beside him.

And it feels like nothing has changed.

We laugh and joke and flirt and let our hands wander until the bottle is finished and we've both passed out in each other's arms.

CHAPTER TWENTY
ROWAN

When I wake up with Circus wrapped around me, my first instinct is to freak the fuck out.

My hangover is a bitch though, and doing anything more than moaning in self-pity seems like too much work.

"Don't panic," Circus hurries to say.

"Panic?" My voice goes up a notch. "Why the hell would I panic?"

He pushes up onto his elbows and looks down at me with sleepy eyes. My focus immediately drops to his lips, and I remember the kisses in vivid detail as though they happened only minutes, not hours ago.

Pressure clamps down on my chest.

"You're panicking."

"No ..." I fight that evil voice back. It's trying to make me feel ashamed. But Circus's face is winning. "I'm ... struggling. I don't want to freak out. I've ..." I pause, not sure how much to tell him. How much pressure would I be putting on him to say he's the first and *only* man I've ever kissed? The first dick I've ever touched?

"So, here's the thing," I say. "Last night ... I've never

done that before."

"Gotten drunk and hooked up with a guy? Shocker."

I want to swat him on the ass, but I can't bring myself to do it. "Kissed a man, other than that one time with you. Touched. Any of it."

His eyebrows creep up. "So what have you done?"

"I've had my dick sucked a couple of times."

Circus bursts out laughing. "Aww, have I popped all your same-sex cherries so far?"

I groan and bury my face. "Maybe not the time for jokes?"

"It's always time for jokes."

I groan again.

Smooth fingers ease my hands back down. "Okay, real talk. You're not allowed to overanalyze. It happened. It was perfectly normal. And it felt incredible. Especially the part where your hand was around my dick."

"You're not going to let me off easy, are you?"

"Hey, I've waited five years for that. I'm going to enjoy it, thanks."

"Yeah ... I'm going to try to."

Circus leans down and leaves a soft kiss on my cheek. "Don't stress. It doesn't have to mean anything. I know where you're at, and I get that it was one of those drunken decisions that probably wouldn't have happened if we were sober. But it did, and it *is* okay. Promise."

I focus on my breathing, just in and out, waiting to see if the disgust is coming. As long as I don't think about it too deeply, I seem to be fine. I'm coping. And each time a flash of a memory sneaks through, I'm reminded of how insanely hot the whole thing was.

And how I want to do it again.

But I'm a lot more sober and one hundred percent more hungover, so it's probably best not to push anything today.

Besides, we leave for LA in a couple of days, I'll have plenty of time to think things through before I go.

A round two or three or whatever seems like an excellent idea now, but the problem is, I'm still no closer to coming out than I was a month ago, so starting something, with someone as special to me as Circus already is, wouldn't be a smart move.

I sit up and the whole room spins as my head gives a massive throb. "Motherfucker."

"You're going already?"

"Yeah. I need to shower. Get yelled at for leaving church. Get questioned about where I spent the night and then get ready for work."

Circus drops back against his pillow and tucks his hands behind his head. "You could ... spend the night again."

His face is so open and hopeful it kills me to turn him down. With my heart in my throat, I lean forward and press a kiss to his forehead. "Not tonight. I'm going to need a little time just to make sure I'm okay. I can't think about anything right now with this headache."

He hurries to nod, and I have no idea how he can manage it after the amount we drank last night. "I'll think of you going through all that pain while I nap the rest of the day away."

"Asshole." I laugh as I nudge him and force myself to stand. Then I glimpse my clothes. "Well, those are for you to deal with." I grab the zebra-print shorts he laid out with a flamingo-patterned shirt. Dear God. Holding in a sigh, I pull them on, adding getting questioned about whose clothes I'm wearing to my list of things to do again.

I turn back when I reach the door, wanting to say more than some lame-ass excuse about how I'm sorry I can't stick around and just enjoy a post-sex morning with him.

How I'm sorry I still have so many issues.

The same issues he had to deal with in high school.

I leave him with a smile, and me with a whole world of regret.

***

"Rowan Alexander Harvey, there you are!"

I've barely stepped foot inside the house when Dad's voice reaches me. I cringe, before turning and making my way into the living area.

Mom, Dad, Grandma, and Grandpa are wearing matching looks of surprise when they see me. And can I blame them?

The buttons on the shirt are still undone, and I couldn't quite get the one on the shorts to fasten. My hair is a mess, my stubble looks untidy, and I'm pretty sure my skin is a sincere shade of green.

And I have zero shits to give.

I need to shower and get the cum out of my pubes because those fuckers pull with every step.

"Where in God's name have you been?" Dad demands.

Here we go. "Out."

They wait.

"Where exactly is out?"

"A friend was having a rough day, so I went to support him."

"Which friend?" Mom asks, rubbing her temples.

And I know I could lie. I know I could throw the name of anyone in town out and they'd believe it. I could tell them it was an old friend from the football team, and my homophobic grandpa would assume only totally straight-guy stuff happened.

"Circus."

And as expected, my grandpa lets out a splutter. "Why on earth were you with someone like him? Is that why you left church yesterday? Are you a sinner now, boy?"

I grit my teeth and try to keep my cool the way Circus did at Leita's barbecue. "Yesterday was the anniversary of his parents' death. I kept him company, we drank too much, and I ..." Okay, *now* for the lie. "I threw up on my clothes, so he lent me some."

"I knew it. Alcohol and parties ..." He rounds on my mom. "See what you let this boy get up to?"

"I'm *not* a boy. I'm a grown-ass man, and if I want to skip out on church to support my friends, you're not going to stop me."

I tear from the room before they can say anything else. And also before I can cry, because all that will do is piss him off more. Crying is for girls.

Motherfucking fuckers.

I slam my door and turn the lock just to make sure no one comes near me. I'm way too hungover for this shit, and the knowledge that I'm going to pay for this later slides down my spine.

Right before I'm hit with the most obscure thought: *What the hell can he do?*

Sure, he throws out mean words and looks down on me and influences all of Mom and Dad's decisions. Grandma will never speak out against him, and if he knew who I really was, I'd probably never see them both again.

It would *hurt*. I know that.

But I also know Leita and Piper well enough to be sure they'd come around. Mom and Dad are the real wild cards. They're the giant question mark that's hanging over my declaration, and honestly, if they turned their backs on me ... that's the part I'm not sure I could get past.

But I'm so. Damn. Tired.

I'm tired of hiding and fighting with myself. I'm tired of not being able to find someone I can fall in love with and plan a future around.

Fueled by my anger, I pull out my phone, pick out one of the photos I took of Circus last night, and take a moment just to appreciate the way my heart gets an extra boost of life at the sight of him.

Imagine what it would be like to have that every day.

And selfishly, I want it.

Waking up next to him this morning was like waking up but realizing you're still dreaming. Even now, it barely feels real.

Though this damn headache has a lot to do with that.

Considering we'll be playing up the whole fake dating thing in LA, I can only imagine our hotel room will have one bed, which means I'm going to get to experience that again, and again, until we come back here.

Again.

To this house.

Where I'm starting to feel distinctly unwelcome.

I stare at the photo for a minute more. His smile, my hand in his hair. I look *happy*.

I upload the photo.

FAKE FRIENDS

Sometimes the answer is staring you in the face.

CHAPTER TWENTY ONE
Circus

I've been to LA a couple of times, but Rowan clearly never has. He's like a dog with his head hanging out of the window, and it makes me laugh to see the sheer enthusiasm. He didn't go silent on me after what happened the other night, which was a total surprise. And when he showed up at my house that night to watch a movie, I couldn't pick my jaw up off the floor.

But he *has* been cagey about what happened at home.

Which is a worry.

That I'm pretending not to think about.

We offload all our stuff at the hotel and take the cab to Preston's office. He's set up a couple of shoots for us before the big one starts tomorrow.

"Circus!" He pulls me into a hug and then turns to Rowan. "And the boyfriend. Well, well. I might not swing that way, but you sure did pick a good one. If we could all look like that, am I right?"

"I'm happy just to look *at* that," I answer.

Rowan looks torn between laughing and walking out of here. And since we're here to play boyfriends, I take full advantage and slide my hand into his.

"Come on, sweetheart. This won't be the last time you're shamelessly checked out today."

We take the elevator to the eleventh floor and step out into the Entertainment Management offices. It's as busy as it always is, and as we cross the foyer, a woman rushes past with a clothing rack.

"Why do I feel like I've stepped onto the set of *The Devil Wears Prada*?"

"Aww ... and somehow people don't know you're gay." I bop him on the nose. "A lot of agencies outsource the photography side of things, but EM keep it all in-house. It was one of the perks that attracted me to signing with Preston in the first place.

"Speaking of ..." Preston says, jumping into the conversation. "Rowan is going to need to sign a contract with me in order to go ahead with the Gucci job."

"A contract?"

"Don't worry, standard stuff. All the same clauses as Circus's, and I've never steered him wrong yet."

Rowan looks uncomfortable. "I'm not looking to do the modeling thing full-time."

"No worries, I can sort out brand placement for your photos. But be aware, that means no slogans, no advertisements, not so much as a water bottle from a competing brand if you're being paid for space on your page."

I squeeze his hand. "It's not as complicated as it

sounds."

"Hmm. Sounds more complicated than I was planning."

"Well, you can thank Circus. I'd already told Gucci you were a solid no and had you written out of the contract."

Uh-oh. I rack my brain, trying to come up with an excuse.

"Sorry, what?"

"He said he wouldn't do this without you, so I had to call my contact and tell them to fire the other model they were about to hire."

I can feel Rowan's eyes on me, and I wait for his questions, but they don't come.

Either he didn't pick up on the awkwardness, or he doesn't care. I'm not about to argue.

Before we start with the photos, Preston drags Rowan into his office to sort out the paperwork. I try to get out of it, but Rowan's grip on my hand is tight and he pulls me through with him.

I almost go cross-eyed listening to it all again. Rowan asks more questions than I ever did, and I swear it takes a lifetime for them to move on from the EM contract to the Gucci one.

"There's a mistake here," Rowan says. "It says the job is worth two hundred thousand, total."

Uh-oh.

Preston quickly checks his copy. "Nope, that's

correct."

Rowan glances at me. "Didn't you say it was two hundred each?"

"Umm …" I pretend like I'm trying to remember. But seriously, who looks at a contract in that much detail? "No, I'm sure I said all up …"

"You didn't." Something seems to dawn on him. "Preston, how much was that swimwear gig worth?"

Preston can clearly tell he's being put on the spot. "Ah, it was …"

I let out a massive sigh. "It was fifty K. All up."

"What the—"

"I don't need the money!"

"And I don't want charity."

"It's not charity, you worked for it. And at that time, I thought you were leaving."

"Is this a fight?" Preston asks.

"No."

Rowan stares at me. "Yes. This is a fight, Circus. You lied."

"Because I knew you wouldn't take it. For fuck's sake, I have more money than I know what to do with, and you know what? When you get that money because your parents died, you start to become really bitter about it. That fifty is yours. The next two hundred, also fucking yours. Don't argue with me on it. I'm not doing this for the money, I'm doing it for the reach and the followers and the opportunities." I fold my arms and turn away from him, not wanting him to see my face.

Yeah, I lied. So what?

The thing is, I *hate* money. I know I'm in the position where I *can* hate it, and I get others aren't so lucky. But it makes me feel sick that every time I look at my bank balance, I'm reminded that it's because of my parents' money that I now have so much.

But fighting with Rowan ... my stomach clenches. Because I'm suddenly realizing that I can't lose him too.

I hear the scratch of a pen as he signs, and then my chair is being dragged backward. Rowan tilts it back so he's looking down at me.

"You okay?"

"Yeah. Are you?"

"I will be." He leans down and kisses my forehead.

Relief sweeps over me.

"Should we do this thing, then get out of here?" he asks.

The chair legs hit the floor, and I get up to bury my face in his chest. He hugs me close, and the anxiety finally loosens.

But the realization hangs on tight.

There are very few people in my life who I actually consider close. People who would do anything for me. Leon is top of that list, followed by Jules and Royce. The other guys are my friends, and they're great, but if I suddenly disappeared, would they really care that much?

With Rowan it's different.

It's not about how much he cares about me, it's about how much I care about *him*.

Because while I'm sure Leon would do anything for me, I'm not so sure Rowan would. Coming out, leaving his family, introducing me to them as *his*, I can't see that ever happening.

But I need him anyway.

The shoot is easier than anything we've done yet. Preston organizes Rowan's portfolio shots first, and then I join him.

Since we're in April, he's got a queer brand lined up with a whole lot of Pride month merch.

"The whole point of these clothes is you're out and you're proud. I want love, guys. We need these to say that people who wear these clothes will find their forever person."

I look up at the exact moment Rowan looks at me.

His stare is intense, and when he reaches a hand out for me, he doesn't drop eye contact. "My forever person, hey?"

"I mean, I'm a real catch. Mommy *and* Daddy issues. Total package."

"I see your issues and raise you family drama." He pulls me into his arms and moves his mouth closer to my ear. "Cock. Balls."

I snort out a laugh. "What are you doing?"

"Whispering sweet nothings into your ear."

"*That's* your version of 'sweet'?"

"Big ol' hairy nuts."

I can't wipe the smile off my face. "You done now?"

"Butthole." He kisses my ear. "Now I am."

We change up the poses, alternating between pretend candid shots and ones that are more staged. And it's easy. I've worked with other models before, but this is intuitive. We read each other and joke around. It doesn't take much to get a real smile, and every time we look at each other, it's easy to pretend that this whole fake thing is real.

Dangerous thoughts.

Because I don't doubt his interest for a minute.

If this were a better world, we'd both be out, and there wouldn't be anything in our way. But as much as I'm starting to feel for him, trying to make a relationship happen while he's still in the closet will be too much for both of us.

It never works.

And I don't know how much longer we can continue pretending like it will.

FAKE FRIENDS

CHAPTER TWENTY TWO
ROWAN

After the shoot, we have the rest of the afternoon off. I'm already tired from all the excitement, but Circus doesn't let me creep back to the hotel to sleep. He insists we do the tourist thing.

I guess we can sleep when we're dead, but that seems like a long way off.

"And look what I brought," Circus says, pulling a Polaroid camera out of his backpack.

I laugh and take it from him as we approach the Hollywood sign. "You know, I don't think I've ever used one of these before."

"I rarely do. But every now and then they're fun to mess around with. I have a bunch of film we can use today, and then another lot for … later."

My ears perk up at his tone. "What's happening later?"

"We're going to be working on your gay comfort levels some more."

Huh. I don't know what to say to that. My dick is letting me know it's on board, but my head still feels funny about it.

Should I be concerned at how easy it is for Circus to be sexual around me?

I shake that thought away. I know it comes from a place I'm trying to ignore. Wanting to get naked as often as possible with Circus isn't because of some loose morals mentality; it's entirely because of how I feel about him. Which is a lot.

And I swear it goes both ways.

Because it's impossible to believe he doesn't feel the same way when he looks at me like that.

He reaches his hand back behind him, and I take it. I let him lead. I'd follow him anywhere.

"Come down here."

We walk down the grassy hill to a point he's happy with. He hesitates a moment, then looks up at me with the most sheepish expression I've ever seen on his face. "Are we okay?"

The lying. When I'd first realized what he'd done, I'd been pissed. It'd made me look stupid, and I felt bad taking his money, but if he can forgive me for something much bigger, forgiving him for this is nothing.

"We're definitely okay. But you can't hide things from me just because it's more convenient. We're, well, *business* partners, I guess. We need to trust each other."

"I get it. But I meant what I said about not wanting the money for this job."

"I don't understand. If you don't like spending your parents' money, why don't you make your own?"

He shrugs and looks out over the valley. "I have, but it all feels tainted now."

I can't imagine what it would be like to lose your parents so young. I hate that he had to go through that. Stepping forward, I pull him closer until I can wrap my arms around him.

"Good pose." He goes to lift the camera, but I take it from his hand.

"No posing. Just let me hug you."

And he does. His hair feels warm against my cheek from the afternoon sun, and he smells like a mixture of the makeup and hair products they used on us.

"Look at you, being all affectionate in public."

I pull back and kiss his temple. "To be fair, it's not like anyone is around."

"Now can I photo?"

Like I'd ever say no to him.

We take nice shots and pull faces, and Circus turns around and pulls his pants down just enough to reveal the top curve of his ass cheeks.

I take the photo quickly, then admire how his warm brown skin looks in the sun.

He catches me staring, and I don't try to hide it.

"You wouldn't be checking me out, would you?"

"Shamelessly."

He winks and pulls his shorts back up. "Come on, then, lots to see."

I swear by the time we're done, it's like he's dragged

me all over the city. All the places have started to blur together, but we've got a pile of Polaroids to refresh my memory. I flick through the pile and pause at the one of Circus's ass. It's a tease of what he's hiding under his clothes. "I'm keeping this one," I tell him as we step into the elevator back to our hotel room.

He laughs. "Oh, honey. There'll be plenty more where that came from."

"Meaning ..."

"Just wait and see."

He takes my hand again, and it's amazing to me how much easier that's become. To hold hands and hug him to me. To let myself feel that rush of nerves, that sweeping high whenever he's around.

All the good that's come from my time with him is making it so hard to believe that loving him could be a bad thing.

"Go and sit on the bed," he directs as soon as we're back in our room.

And like every time we've taken photos together, I'm obedient.

I kick off my shoes, dump my things on the bedside table, and then sit back against the pillows.

Circus tosses the camera onto the bed beside me.

"The only rule is, no touching."

"Wha—"

He reaches up and slowly starts to unbutton his shirt. We both watch his long slim fingers as they move, and then Circus glances up and hooks me in his stare. "Are you just going to sit there and look at me? Or are you going to work?"

Work ... I look at the camera, and what he's planning makes sense. This isn't going to be like any shoot we've done before.

I take a deep breath and meet his eyes again. "Keep going."

Then I start to take photos.

The hint of his chest through his open shirt.

Click.

The bare plains of his back as he lets his shirt slowly slip down his arms.

Click.

That delicious V that curves over his hips and disappears from sight.

Click.

I lick my lips as he exposes more and more skin, pretending as though I'm not here. And he knows how to work the camera. Every angle makes his body look like art, and I'm glad he made the no-touching rule clear, because my hands are itching to reach for him.

He pops the button on his shorts, and I suck in a breath. Hold it. Watch greedily as he turns his back to me again. His thumbs slide under the waistband of his shorts, and he slowly pushes them from his hips and down over his thighs.

I remember to breathe.

To take another photo.

And when Circus turns back to face me, the erection straining at his briefs tells me he's just as turned on as I am.

He poses a few more times before he gets to work on what I'm waiting for. He runs a hand over his cock, before reaching for his underwear. And when he starts to push them down, he catches my eyes again.

I can't look away until his eyes fall shut and he straightens, arms hooked over his head and angry red dick on full display.

It's the first time I've seen it properly. Sober. No drunken haze. And I commit the sight to memory before I lift the camera again.

"You're so fucking sexy," I breathe. I'm beginning to get concerned I'm going to come in my underwear again. And considering I'm not a teenager anymore, I'd prefer to avoid a repeat performance.

I stand up. "Get on the bed."

He does as I say, tight body moving so fluidly as he crawls onto the mattress and slides forward to lie on his stomach.

And he better have a shitload of film for this thing because I'm prepared to take photos all night. My breathing is so heavy it fills the otherwise quiet room.

"On your back."

He rolls over. One arms rests above his head while the other runs slowly from his chest, down his tight stomach to rest on his cock.

"Stroke yourself."

Seeing him follow every direction I give him is beautiful. I'm so turned on I can barely think straight, and the fly of my jeans is pressing painfully against my dick. I'm a little scared to suggest it, but I need to get naked.

"I want one more, then it's your turn. Roll back over. Leave your face on the bed, and get up on your knees."

Heat burns in his expression as he watches me for a second. Then he does exactly as I've asked. I watch the deep groove of his spine move sensually as he rolls onto his front, and when he pushes to his knees—

"Holy shit I wanna touch ..." I lift the camera, noticing my hands have finally started to shake. But there isn't an ounce of fear standing in my way, only lust so heavy and deep I could sob.

I greedily drink in the sight of him open and exposed for me, putting himself on full display in possibly the most vulnerable state I can imagine.

My eyes roam from his hole, along his taint, to where his balls are hanging heavy between his legs.

OhGodIneedtotouch ...

I take a photo from the back, from the side, then climb onto the bed on my knees and take one of the way his waist dips in before flaring out to his round ass.

Then I drop the camera beside him.

Circus takes photos of me as I start to undress, and

when I finally drop my briefs to the floor and wrap my hand around my cock, it's instant relief.

My moan tears from me.

"Lie down, spread your legs, and jerk yourself off." I do it automatically, because it's easier to follow directions than try and think right now, and with every click and whirl of each photo, I'm able to block the sound out.

All the teasing, all the photos, all the views of Circus's body have me aching and needy and more ready to come than I ever have been in my life.

My hand moves faster, and I'm barely aware of Circus moving around the room until a heavy *thump* hits the mattress beside me.

"Shoot is over," he says, voice even huskier than usual. Then he leans down, looks me straight in the eye, and says, "Now I'm going to suck your cock."

The sound that leaves me isn't actually human and definitely not intelligible. I snatch my hand away from my dick and watch as Circus bends down and wraps his lips around it.

The heat, the suction ... it has to be the greatest feeling that exists in the world, and my cock is in heaven.

It's instant relief to the insane aching, and as Circus picks up his pace, I wrap my hand through his hair and grip tight. He works me over like no one's ever done before, and I can't stop my hips from thrusting up to meet him.

My mind is a complete buzz of pressure, wiped clean from every other thought I've ever had, and when Circus takes the entire length in his mouth, it's all over.

My orgasm crashes into me, and it's a good thing I'm lying down because I'm not so sure my legs would hold with the way I'm shaking.

Before I can recover, before I can take a moment to let the thoughts creep back in, I tackle Circus onto the bed, slide down his body, and wrap my lips around the head of his dick.

He's already leaking, and the precum tastes kind of salty. I have no idea what I'm doing, but all I know is I'm done being a twenty-four-year-old gay man who's never had the taste of cock on his tongue.

I shut down the voices trying to push through now that my brain isn't humming with pleasure and focus on being present and making this as good for Circus as I can.

I moan as I work him deeper, sucking and bobbing and rolling his balls in my palms, until my dick starts to perk up again.

But this isn't about me.

This is how that first blow job he gave me should have gone. I should have pushed him into one of the classrooms and returned the favor, but back then, the voices were too loud.

Here, now, he's consumed me, leaving almost no room for anything else.

"Rowan ... fuck, Rowan, I'm going to come."

I pull back a little, and the feel of his cum hitting the back of my throat makes me gag. I try to swallow as much of it as I can, but I clearly need a lot more practice because we both end up a complete mess.

Circus slowly sits up and pulls my face up to meet his.

When he kisses me, I swear the world stops.

CHAPTER TWENTY THREE
CIRCUS

He hasn't let me go. Not even to clean up the mess he left behind.

And I'm not complaining.

But I am wondering what's going through his head.

So far he's just hugged me tight, all wrapped around my body as he presses soft kisses to my shoulder or my collarbone or my neck.

I let my fingers trail down his back, trying to enjoy the moment and not worry about what happens when the panic kicks in.

"Your thoughts are loud," he grumbles, then hooks his leg over my waist and rolls on top of me. "What's going on?"

I don't know whether to say, but he's way ahead of me.

"You're waiting for me to freak out."

"Obviously."

He brushes my hair back from my forehead. "That was ..." His brown eyebrows bunch together and relax just as quickly. "I didn't have time to think. It was more instinctual than anything, like I wasn't fully in control, so my brain didn't get a chance to second-guess anything."

"And now?"

He drops his head onto my shoulder. "It's hard. Like I'm fighting with myself. But every time I start to have doubts and worry, I remind myself that nothing's ever felt like that. Ever. I've ..." Rowan hesitates.

"Keep going."

His exhale comes out in a rush. "I've had sex with women before. I didn't enjoy it. And afterward, I hated myself for it. So much that a couple of times I thought it might just be better to end it."

"Jesus ..."

"I'm okay," he rushes to add, and at least his smile seems genuine. "I just hated myself so much. I hated that I couldn't be like other men. When I first booked in with my psychologist, it was because I was hoping she could help me find a way to suppress it. To find women more attractive."

It doesn't work like that. And if anyone suggested it, I'd laugh in their faces. But Rowan was clearly hurting, and I can't imagine how desperate he would have to have been in order to try and force himself to be with people he wasn't into.

"She helped me through most of my issues, except the regret I felt about you. And now being here with you and letting myself finally start to experience what I've held back for so long feels inherently *wrong*. Like the ground has suddenly disappeared and I'm scrambling for something to hold on to."

My gut twists.

"But I don't want to be that way. And every time we're together, every time I push myself, it gets that little bit easier. So if I'm quiet or withdrawn after sex, I swear it's nothing to do with you."

"Thank you." I run my fingers down Rowan's face, and he ducks his head to kiss me.

It's lazy and sweet and all I need right now. He pulls away and settles on my chest, tattooed arms snaking around me.

"I don't know what I'm going to do about my family."

"Do you think …" I hold my breath. "Do you think you'll ever tell them?"

"Honestly … I can't see me having the balls to do it. Which is a cop-out, I know. And I'm sure it's probably the last thing you want to hear right now."

I card my fingers through his hair and hold him tighter. "Don't worry about what I want. If you can't tell them, that's your choice, and *only* your choice."

"But I *want* to." Frustration seeps into his voice. "It's bullshit I can't say two little words."

I want to push him. Or tell him to stop being a wimp. "I know what it's like to lose my family," I tell him. "And if you have a chance to hold on to yours, I'd never hold that against you."

"I have been thinking though …"

"About?"

"Well, what if I didn't have to tell them?"

"And be closeted for the rest of your life?"

"Sort of." His pause stretches out between us, but I can tell there's more. "I need a little more distance from my family. I was talking to Leon about how Sunbury needs a gym and thought that would be an awesome thing for me to pursue. I could run classes and train people who wanted it … and Sunbury isn't a huge town, so I know it's not something that would rake in the profits, but as long as I could take a wage, I'd be fine. And I'd be doing something I love instead of working at Harvey's."

His voice has increased, strengthened, and it makes me happy to hear him excited about this. "What does that have to do with your family?"

"With my own income, I could get my own place, and then I wouldn't be reliant on them at all. It means I'd be able to take my own risks. Hang out with who I want to hang out with." He shifts and meets my eyes. "Maybe find myself a male *roommate* one day."

It kills me to have to break his enthusiasm. "That plan sounds perfect, except for one part."

"Which is?"

"Asking someone you love to pretend to be your roommate isn't fair. It'd be like forcing them back into the closet."

He's quick to shake his head. "We wouldn't be

closeted to our friends or the people who know us."

"Oh really? So you'd hold his hand walking down O'Connell Road? You'd get married and not invite your parents? And what if he wants children one day? What? You and your roommate just adopted some kids together?"

His forehead creases.

"I'm sorry." And I am. The last thing I want to do is give him a dose of reality when he's actually starting to think of a future for himself. "But I know what it's like to sit at a table and eat dinner with your family and to just be there as your 'friend.' Rowan, it sucks. And that was in high school when nothing had even happened except for the flirting and all those near kisses. That was all childish stuff and now ..." I cover my face with my hand. "It would kill me now."

I feel Rowan push up onto his forearms, and I'm acutely aware of him looking down at me. "W-why is it different now?"

"Huh?"

"Why would it kill you now? What's changed?"

I think I'm falling in love with you. Which I certainly cannot fucking say to his face. I shouldn't even be thinking that when his solution for living as a gay man is having a *roommate*. That one hundred percent isn't something I will do. "We've had sex. That always changes the dynamic."

I know it's not the answer he wanted. And if I'd

asked him that same question, I'm almost certain he would have said what I was thinking. These feelings have gone further than either of us ever intended them to, and when I'd been imagining an explosion, I'd thought it would be our relationship that blew up. Not my heart.

"Fair enough." He settles beside me and rolls my body so I'm facing him. "Well, I've just spilled my guts about my problem. What are you going to do about yours?"

"What problem?"

Rowan gives me a soft look. "Anyone would be as upset about losing their parents. I can't even imagine. But the money thing. Building a big house for, and I quote, 'a whole bunch of kids.' Wanting a family but not wanting to put yourself out there. I mean, fuck. You're here with me. Someone who'll probably be closeted until he's an old man. You should be finding someone you can settle down with."

I don't know why, after everything he just said, that's the most painful part. Suggesting I leave what we have—which admittedly, isn't much—and find someone else makes me want to hit something.

"Plus the social media," he continues.

"What about it?"

He pins me with a serious look. "I've been following your account for years. You think I haven't noticed the way certain photos suddenly disappear? And since I've been back, you're constantly checking your phone, and talking about interactions, and assessing the shots we put up and how they'll be received."

"It's called business."

"You're lonely."

I go to sit up, planning to, I don't know ... shower, throw myself off a ledge? Anything to get out of this conversation.

"No, you don't," Rowan says, hooking his arm around my waist and pinning me against the bed. "I'm just saying, it wouldn't be a terrible thing for you to see someone."

I glare at him. "When you have no one, you tell me how open you'd be to talking to someone about that. To admitting that the two people in the world who actually love you are gone, and now you're just sitting back, watching your friends find their partners and live their lives and spend their holidays with their families."

He laughs a little. "Circus, you live your life more than anyone I know. You're creative and talented. You go out and experience the world. And you have friends who love you. So what, you haven't found your forever person yet. You would have to be the easiest person to love because you accept people for who they are. You understand them." Rowan cups my face and steers it so he can meet my eyes. "And until you find that person, I'm going to spend all my holidays with you. Every one of them. We'll visit my nephews and spoil them with presents on Christmas. We'll have your friends over for

Easter, and I'll bake a whole vat load of chocolate brownies, and we'll feed everyone until their stomachs burst. Thanksgiving we'll spend just the two of us. And we'll have a turkey and be quiet and think about the people who should be there with us." His eyes turn soft, and I'm sure he's about to cry. "And on Mother's and Father's Day ... we'll go visit them. Together. I'll hold you while you cry and, Jesus, I'll probably cry too."

I swallow around the lump forming in my throat as my eyes start to prickle. "What about your family?"

"I'll see them the days in between. But holidays, those are yours now."

I laugh because if I don't, I'll cry. "And if they think there's something going on with us?"

The first bit of uncertainty seeps into his expression. Then he smiles. "I'll tell them you're my roommate." Rowan starts to tickle me, and I snort while I bat him away.

"Fine. Deal. Your holidays are all mine."

He kisses me softly. "Looking forward to it."

CHAPTER TWENTY FOUR
ROWAN

The Gucci photoshoot is huge. A massive set, lights everywhere, racks and racks of clothes. No one talks to us much, and there's a lot of standing around and waiting.

We're shuffled on for certain shots, staged, told to hold awkward poses that make my muscles burn.

Not only are there photos, but we also have to stage behind-the-scenes "scenes" where we're laughing and having fun and sneaking secret moments between shots to hug and share kisses.

It's all bullshit. I know this isn't something I'd be able to do with my life long term. It's a fun ride, a bit of a thrill. But if Circus wasn't here with me, I probably would have walked out by now.

It takes three days to get all the shots they need, and as soon as we're out of there each day, Circus drags us to dinner or a show, and then we go back to the hotel room and fool around.

I could endure just about anything to end up in bed with him.

When we finally wrap on the final day, and I change out of the stiff, uncomfortable clothing, there's champagne passed around.

We both wave them off, keen to get on the road. Neither of us are in a huge hurry to get back to Sunbury, so we've set aside a week to do the fourteen-hour drive. There are plenty of places to stop along the way that Circus says will be good for aesthetics.

I can't believe I actually know what that means now.

And after four days of being inside, I'm glad to get out of the city. We stop at Redwood Park and freshwater lagoons, and Circus is always there with his camera. We went through all the Polaroid film on our first night in LA, but I'm definitely up for a repeat at some point in the future.

That's if we're still doing this when we get back.

It's been a bit of a mindfuck. Acting like boyfriends during the day and then making each other come at night. My brain is struggling to keep up with the difference between what's real and what's still pretend.

Could I ask Circus? Of course. But do I trust him to give me a straight answer? Not so much.

The thing I'm most scared of though will be Circus telling me this is over when we get back. I'm becoming more at ease with touching him and letting myself go, and if he decides that's all I needed, I'm not so sure I could keep playing happy boyfriends for him in front of the camera.

Because Circus is someone special.

Even if he doesn't see it, I've known since I was

sixteen years old and trying to catch his eye.

I don't want to let him go. Not now.

Maybe not ever.

And isn't that a scary thought?

Because the more I think about it, the more he's right that I could never ask someone as special to me as he is to pretend to be my roommate. Our friends would know, but who else? If I don't want my family finding out, that pretty much excludes everyone else in town. It's too risky otherwise.

Damn, I want him though. More than just his body. I want his heart. I want him to know that *we* can be a family.

I sigh as Circus pulls up to the edge of a creek.

"Where are we?"

"Figured we'd stay here tonight."

"And be killed by a mass murderer? Sounds like a solid plan."

He laughs. "What is it about you and forests? You realize we're more likely to be found and killed in the middle of a city. Who else is out here, huh?"

I lean closer to him. "That's the question of the night."

Ignoring all sense of self-preservation, he jumps out and heads around to the back of the car. I reluctantly follow him. He's got a stack of blankets and pillows piled up back here, and he offloads our luggage to the front seats before starting to set up.

"You had this planned, didn't you?"

"Why do you think I rented an SUV?"

"It's going to be impossible to sleep back here."

He reaches up to kiss me. "Who says we're going to be sleeping?"

"Ah. Not just a pretty face."

He crawls in first, and I pull off my shirt and follow him. Dusk has set in, staining the trees around us in an orange glow. Circus snuggles into my side, and as much as I might want to jump his bones, I'm also completely content right here. Until he pulls out the photos of the other night.

"I want to post some," he says, and my face must go white or something because he starts to laugh.

"I don't think ..."

He holds one up of me jerking off. "Nothing like this. These are mine." He flicks through the pile and finds one where he's facedown, naked, and looking like he's asleep. "Maybe this?" He starts to drop a few down. One where we're cuddling, one of me with my thumbs hooked in my briefs, and another of me standing with my back to the camera, ass on full display.

I shift a little. "Everything we've done so far ... I could explain it away as just modeling. All pretend. These ..." Everything from our lack of clothes to the expressions we're wearing hint at total intimacy. "They're private. I want these to be ours. For us to just have this. No one else."

At first, I'm sure he's going to argue. And okay, there are some photos here we could definitely get away with, but I'm oddly protective of that night.

"What if we post some from during the day instead? There were a few of those you loved."

"You're right." He gathers the pile he laid out, and I take them from him.

"I hope you know I'm keeping all the ones of you. *All* of them."

"That's fine because I want to be able to see your dick anytime I want, so I'll be keeping yours too."

I laugh as he slides one of my naked photos from the pile and flops back on the blankets.

"Ooh, Rowan. Look at you and your big cock…" He pretends to lick the photo.

I pluck it out of his hand and place it back on the pile. "You know…" I'm not sure now is the time for this conversation, but we might as well have it anyway. "You could see it anytime you wanted, even without the photos."

"Like right now."

I laugh. "Yes, in a minute."

Circus pouts. "But you said whenever I wanted, and I want to now."

"Hey." I catch his hand as he reaches for my pants. "Give me a second. I'm trying to say that once we get back, I wouldn't mind if this keeps happening."

He looks torn. I'm not surprised, because when it

comes down to it, I don't have a whole lot to offer him.

"You could help me with my gym," I continue. "And I'll keep posting and you'll keep getting your followers and we'll spend time together, and at night, we'll keep each other company." I swallow. "Until you find someone who can give you everything you deserve."

"You want to be my little sex toy?" Circus asks, raspy voice even scratchier than usual.

"Hell yes …" And more. But that more part can stay with me until I can—if ever—give him an actual life with me.

I reach for Circus's shirt and pull it over his head before leaning down and kissing him. I take my time, exploring his mouth with my tongue, and just sinking into the feel of him against me. All I can do is hope and pray that he doesn't find someone special in the time it takes for me to get my shit together.

I hum against his mouth as he pushes my pants down, and then I roll over and pull him on top of me. I hurry to flick open the button on his pants and let my hands trail over his ass as I push them down.

"You sure no one will come out this way?"

"Nope." He ducks his head to drag openmouthed kisses over my neck. "You want to stop?"

"I don't think I'd want to stop even if there were crowds of people." A moan rumbles in my chest as he sucks a mark into my skin.

I pull him tighter against me and slide my hand

down the back of his briefs, running my middle finger down the crease of his ass.

Circus pulls back and looks down at me. "Would you …"

"Would I …?"

"Fuck me?"

My face gets so hot I can't concentrate. The thought of sliding into his body, owning it, making him come while he rides me … "Yes. Yes, yes. So much yes."

"Really?" The way his face lights up surprises me.

The thing is there are still doubts there. Some worries that I'll never be enough. That I'll get home and chicken out and force myself through dating women again.

But then I look at him.

His bedroom eyes and the sharp line of his jaw. His septum piercing and his long eyebrows and the way his dark hair gets that wave at the front.

Nothing and no one will ever compare to him. I drag my lips softly against his. "Really."

Circus kicks out of his underwear, then scrambles out of the car and jogs to the driver's side door. He's back in a minute with a wide smile and two little packets between his fingers.

"Smart man," I say.

"The smartest."

He climbs back into the car, and I sit up a little so I'm propped against the back seats. As soon as he's close enough, my hands find his waist and I steer him to straddle my lap.

We kiss while he grinds against me, my hands exploring every part of him I can reach. I trail a hand back down to his ass, and Circus pulls away to grab one of the packets.

"Here."

He grabs my hand and pours a little of the lube onto my fingers, then does the same with his own.

"Follow the leader." He grins wickedly, then reaches around, and I hurry to follow suit. And when I feel what his hand is doing, my cock gives a massive throb.

I cup his hand and groan as one of his fingers pushes inside his hole.

"Fuck. You're fingering yourself."

"Mmhmm ... help me."

Porn has taught me the basics of what's expected, but I have *no* clue what to do now I'm confronted with the reality of it.

Circus slides out a bit, and I link my fingers through his, leaving one out to rest alongside the one he's riding. And when he starts to push both fingers back inside himself ...

The pressure is insane.

He works himself up to three fingers, stretching himself out, and then he starts to rub something.

"Feel that?" he asks, face cloudy with lust.

"Yeah. Is that your prostate?"

"Sure is." He tilts my head back with his free hand and forces his tongue deep into my mouth. We kiss until I'm close to running out of air, and then he backs up, removing our digits from his ass.

I grab the condom, tear open the packet, and hurry to roll it down my aching dick. Circus covers it with the leftover lube, and I moan as his hand strokes me.

I catch his hips before he can move.

"I've ... I've never had sex before that I enjoyed. If I'm weird after ..."

He lightly ghosts his lips over mine. "I'll be here."

I let out a shuddery breath as Circus positions himself over me. "You ready?"

"Very." I wrap my arms around his back and ease him down.

Circus holds my cock steady, and the first moment I breach his hole is insane. I've never felt anything so tight and hot.

My mouth immediately seeks out his as he slides farther down.

And everything, everything has been building to this moment.

From the first glance of him in the halls, to meeting for lunches, then catching up after school. From the way I'd stare at the back of his head in church, just waiting for that moment he'd turn around so we could lock eyes.

Sneaking into his prom. Our first kiss. The years between where I've been dying to get back to him.

It's not just the pressure around my cock that's building to insane levels, but the one around my heart too.

His ass hits my hips, and then he sits there for a moment, both of us panting into each other's mouths. It's perfection.

It's too much.

He starts to move, and I swear my eyes roll back in my head. This. *This* is everything I've been missing.

I slide my hands down to grip his ass and increase the pace, but it's not enough. I need more control. More access.

Wrapping my arms around him, I flip Circus onto his back and slide into his waiting hole. It's just as amazing the second time.

I don't hold back.

I unleash years of pent-up emotion on him.

Circus's head is tilted back, eyes closed, denying me from seeing him, so I reach up and grab his face. "Look at me."

His eyes snap open. "Use me," he pants.

My fingers tighten on his jaw as I start to slam into him, hips taking on a mind of their own. We don't break eye contact, not even when my orgasm starts to build. Not even when my balls draw up tight and I'm hanging in that moment between bliss and total loss of control.

"Kelly ..." I gasp.

He scrambles to reach between us, and his eyelids

sink heavy over his eyes as he madly jerks himself off. "Fuck, fuck, *fuck*."

Cum spurts between us, and that's enough to send me over the edge. My high hits hard and fast, and the whole time I'm riding it out, all I can concentrate on are the warm, soft feelings flooding through my body.

This is what it's meant to be.

Pure attraction. No regrets. Sex with the person I love.

I collapse on top of him, hiding my face in his neck as I struggle against tears.

My mind completely blown apart.

Nothing will ever compare to this moment.

And goddamn it, I don't want to be the guy who cries after sex, but it all gets too much. I've denied myself this for years, and for what?

Some outdated ideas and the promise of eternity in hell?

Fuck it. At this point, I don't want to be separated from Circus, ever.

Circus hugs me close, waiting while I cry, and I wish I could tell him what this means to me. The sex, his support, all of it.

Is it really any surprise why I've fallen in love with him?

"You did so good," he murmurs against my ear. "So good."

"I'm sorry," I reply, wishing I could stop my damn

eyes from leaking.

"Don't be." His hold makes me feel safe. "We have plenty of time. And tomorrow night, we can practice this all again."

CHAPTER TWENTY FIVE
CIRCUS

I basically have a boyfriend.

And I say *basically* because we haven't discussed anything official and probably never will, but I'm coming to terms with the fact that no one but Rowan will do.

I want him for holidays.

I want him in my bed at night.

I want him in my photos online and in my house when it gets too quiet.

I want him to fill my afternoons and start my mornings.

I just want ... *him*.

Which makes me a gigantic idiot.

Maybe I should be called "jester" instead because my life is one big joke.

Sorry, Mom and Dad. I've given up who I am for a man.

The whole way back to Sunbury is a dream. Just me and him, stopping and driving and fucking whenever we want. It's incredible, and I can't help picture life like this always.

Fun through the day, and him making love to me at

night.

And that's exactly what he does.

I've been fucked before. I've fucked others before. I have never *made love*, but Rowan shows me why it's called that, even if we've never said the word.

The passion and care and burst of emotion he sets off every time is my new weakness.

We drop the rental car in Portland, and Leon picks us up for the rest of the drive home.

It's late afternoon before we arrive back in Sunbury and drop Rowan at his parents' place. I want to kiss him goodbye but know it isn't possible, and I can tell by the look he gives me that he feels the same.

He brushes his thumb over my cheek, grabs his bags, and leaves.

I let out a long breath as Leon pulls away from his house.

"You okay?"

"No …" I turn to him, and I'm sure I must look pitiful. "I'm in love."

Leon starts to laugh. "Goddamn, Circus …"

"I know."

"You're an idiot."

"I *know*."

Leon steers the truck down O'Connell Road, heading toward my place. "So what are you planning on doing about it?"

I scratch my ear. "He, umm … He's planning on

opening a gym. And moving out to his own place, then—and I know this is dumb—but then when he finds someone, he thinks he can tell his parents he's got a roommate ..." I trail off at the look on Leon's face.

"For the love of God, please tell me you're not going to offer to be that roommate."

"Well, what am I supposed to do? He won't come out. I want to be with him. This gives me a way."

"Nope." Leon shakes his head. "Because his family aren't idiots. Bigots, yes. Idiots, no. If you do this, they'll work it out eventually, and how will you feel if he's forced to come out because of you? How will *he* feel if his family abandon him because of *you*?"

I hate it when Leon's right.

"You have any thoughts?"

"I do, but they're way too logical for where you're at right now."

"Okay, then what are your thoughts for how I can make this happen?"

Leon starts to laugh. "I have zero clue. If he won't come out ... I don't know. Do the roommates thing if you want, but don't be surprised when you're in a mess that can't be fixed."

My best friend, lords and lads.

He drops me off, and I walk inside my large, empty house.

I don't know what I was thinking. All this space with no one to share it with? I'm a headcase.

And I hate to say it, but I think I do need to speak with someone.

Rowan wouldn't have made the massive improvements he has if it wasn't for admitting he needed help.

I mean yeah, probably not the *right* kind of help, but he got there in the end.

I pace through to my living room and try to imagine the high ceilings hung with garlands of holly. An enormous Christmas tree in front of the windows and the smell of pine needles and hot cocoa filling the room.

For the first time since I started thinking about a family of my own, I finally have a face I can picture here with me.

I might not have wanted to end up here with Rowan, but I'm in it now. No point whining and doing the denial thing because trying to keep my distance will only hurt us both. And hurting Rowan is the last thing I want.

So if I can't turn these feelings off, and I'm not going to walk away, I have to find a way to make this work.

Because Leon's right, roommates isn't an option.

Think that will stop me though?

The idea of having Thanksgiving here, just the two of us, fills me with so much need it's probably unhealthy to attribute it to one person. Then I imagine the table full of food and all my friends around it, and I can see it so clearly, I'm desperate for it to happen.

So. Plan.

My office is a small room off the studio, and I only use it for conference calls or to do my taxes. Other than the extra bedrooms, it's maybe the least used room in the house.

There are three things I need to work out.

First, Rowan wants to start a gym.

Second, he needs out of that house.

And third, what can I contribute?

Now we've done those jobs he doesn't need money. He could buy a small apartment in town easily. But ...

I also have a *lot* of rooms.

My common sense is screaming at me to put that thought back in its box, but would it be that unbelievable if I asked him?

He could put the money he has into his business.

There's *so* much extra space here, and if I get what I want, he'll be here with me most of the time anyway.

Still, it's a lot to put on such a new relationship.

Especially when we're going to have enough to face as it is.

I shake my head. Okay, first point. The gym.

I have a storefront I lease from a man on O'Connell Road that would be a convenient option. With that kind of prime real estate, it wouldn't take much to get the word out. And with the Summer Nights Festival less than a month away, it would be a good time to launch. But ... that means nowhere to display my pictures like I normally do at the festivals. I would have liked to include some of Rowan this year.

That said, it's not like I need the money, and I can probably just bite the bullet and set up an online store like I've been thinking of doing for a while now. It's always been my way of getting into the town spirit.

Now, maybe I can do that by helping Rowan.

I spend the afternoon working out how much the equipment and rent and insurances will cost. There's a lot more that goes into a business beyond throwing up some pretty pictures, and I research it all.

Maybe the shock of being home will remind Rowan why he's always kept his distance from men. Maybe Leita will successfully get him involved with one of her single friends, who he can hide behind until he's an old man.

Or maybe we'll find a way to make this work so we both get what we want.

I don't even know.

But if I keep pretending like everything is fine, I'll will it into existence.

Right?

Right.

I've got this all under control.

So long as I ignore the closeted aspect.

And the uncertainty.

And that lingering voice in Rowan's head that's determined to sabotage everything for him.

Not to mention my truckload of issues.

I pull a face at my computer screen as I lean back in

my chair.
    Yep.
    Everything.
    Is.
    Fine.

FAKE FRIENDS

CHAPTER TWENTY SIX
ROWAN

The loud creak of the front door echoes loudly in the hall. If anyone's home, they'll know I'm here in about a minute, but I'm not in the mood to face them.

I didn't bother telling anyone where I went for a reason. I didn't want the questioning, and I didn't want them to try and guilt me out of going once they knew Circus was involved.

So I left them a note saying I'd be gone a couple of days and then texted Mom that it would be a couple of days more.

And damn were they good days.

I dump my bag on the bed, tempted to pull the Polaroids out, just to remind myself that day happened. In this house though, that'd be a recipe for disaster, so instead of listening to my instincts, I start looking for a good hiding place.

There's a knock at my door, and I quickly shove my whole bag in the closet before the door starts to open.

Mom pokes her head inside.

"I thought that was you," she says, walking closer to pull me into a hug. "How was your time away?"

"Yeah, good. Didn't miss me too much at the diner?"

"I'll always miss you, but the diner was fine."

I smile, really hoping she means that.

"You picked a good night to get back. Piper's coming over for dinner, so Gran cooked her cheesy chili bake and apple pie. And we all know how much you love her pie."

"It's like you knew I'd be here for it."

She taps her temple. "A mother's intuition. Now get changed, dinner's nearly ready."

Pity her mother's intuition missed a pretty big thing about me. If she'd just *known*, it would have made a world of difference.

If I couldn't hide the gay, I'd already be outed and therefore I'd already know the outcome.

It's the not knowing that's driving me crazy.

It's the wanting to be with Circus, so much, that I'm actually for the first time in my entire life tossing up just how bad things could get—and whether it would be worth the trade-off.

Mom leaves me to unpack my shit, and I finally stash the photos away where I'm sure no one will accidentally find them. Now, if they were to purposely go looking for some big, gay contraband they'd probably sniff them out quickly, but while my family are a lot of things, they're not snoops.

I've just put a load of washing on when I hear Piper arrive, but even still, I drag my feet.

When I imagine family, I picture warmth and love

and acceptance, and I wish I could claim that was because my own family empowered me to think that way, but unfortunately, mass media consumption has more to do with that impression.

My family are warm in their own way. But when it comes to Grandpa and his opinions, it's fall in line or leave.

It constantly makes me wonder whether Mom and Dad just do the church thing for him or if they actually believe it themselves.

Not that it matters.

After going to church for so long, it's hard to get those teachings out of your head. And while I have to admit there *is* a lot of good in there, it also comes with a heavy undercurrent of obedience and compliance which I'm not so comfortable with.

Some days I wish there were an off switch for religion.

But without one, I just have to hope my parents' love is stronger than the voices the church leaves in your head.

And I know firsthand how loud those voices are.

I sigh and run a hand through my dirty hair, figuring I should probably take an actual shower after a week of bathing in ponds or whatever off-road dingy motel we could find.

Then I guess I can't put off facing them any longer.

I'm too jittery to enjoy my shower, so I scrub quickly

and get out, dress, and decide I might as well get all the questioning over with.

I can never tell them the whole truth, but I'm not going to lie about who I was with.

So if they ask, it's on them.

I'm surprised Mom didn't give me the third degree the second I walked in the door.

"Ah, he is alive," Grandpa says dryly, the moment I walk into the living area. "Here we were thinking you'd run away again."

All I have to do is keep my cool. "I didn't run away the first time, I went to college. Big difference." I quickly turn my attention to my sister, swamping her in a hug. "Piper, blessing us with your company, huh?"

She snorts. "Hardly. It's more like *I* wanted company."

And like she's said the magic words, the heat immediately passes from me to her. I'd feel bad, but ... I don't.

"You just need to find yourself a husband," Gran says. "Once you have a man in your life, you won't feel so lonely."

I wonder if she'd give me the same advice.

"Yeah," I agree, and Piper frowns at me. "Or a dog. A hamster. Maybe one of those descented skunks."

Her frown deepens. "Or I could just visit my family and not transfer my emotions onto another being."

Gran sniffs, and I know she's immediately about to

launch into her *you're getting older* bit. "Don't leave it too long, Piper. You're a beautiful girl now, but in a few years ..." Right on cue.

And instead of just taking it like she normally would, Piper bites back. "Well, you'll excuse me if the guy I liked decided he'd rather go *gay* than date me. Sorry, Gran, that must be so disappointing for you."

Yikes. There's a definite tone there I'm not liking. It has me torn between pointing out Tanner is bi and he and Royce were always going to happen, and keeping quiet. Because if there's one thing I've always relied on, it's knowing my sisters will have my back. But can I count on that when she's holding on to this resentment?

Grandpa waves his hand. "I swear the gays are everywhere these days."

"We pray for them, you know," Gran says.

And that's more than enough for me. I get up to go check if Mom needs any help in the kitchen, but she meets me in the doorway.

"Dinner's served," she calls, ushering me toward my seat. Which means no getting away from any of them.

It's stifling. The tiny dining room, bumping elbows with Piper at the six-seater table. Sitting directly opposite Gran and right next to Grandpa.

And yet it's like I'm worlds apart.

They're all talking like there isn't a gigantic wall between me and them, and they cover off every mundane topic from town gossip to how Harvey's is going.

And I should care. I should enjoy this with them. But after spending so much time with Circus, and letting myself feel what I've been running from for years, I don't *want* to keep it all in. I want to share that I'm happy and possibly in love.

It fucking sucks that I can't.

Gran's chili usually helps boost my spirits, but even it's not enough to distract me. I glance over at where Piper's pushing her food around the plate, and I guess I'm not the only one going through emotional stuff. Is she still upset over Tanner? And if she is, am I breaking some kind of sibling code by being friends with him?

I nudge Piper with my elbow and pitch my voice low. "I've been thinking about the diner and how you've been looking for new ideas. Ever thought of adding something vegetarian to the menu?"

A light smile crosses her lips, but before she can answer, Dad cuts her off. "Vegetarian options cost too much in overhead and wastage. There's no market for it."

Apparently I didn't speak quietly enough. "We make everything to order anyway, why don't we just let people choose what they want?"

"Then you create the habit of people changing everything just because they can. You'll have custom orders coming out of your ears and be unable to keep up. The way we do it now is a process we've perfected over years, and it works."

My jaw ticks as I clench my teeth.

There's no point arguing. But apparently Piper thinks there is. "Actually, it'll make us more competitive. We're still pulling a steady profit with our regulars, but we rarely see new people through the doors. I'm there every day, and I pay attention. Changing some things up wouldn't be a terrible idea. I mean, look at Peg's. That place is constantly full. And if we sit around just relying on our current business, that business will eventually dry up."

Dad's eyes flick toward Grandpa, and it's so subtle I almost miss it. But as usual, he's worried about saying the wrong thing.

I watch as Grandpa knocks his veiny knuckles against the table, then sighs. "Well, just take a look at Tanner Everett. If he's not a sign that times are changing, I don't know what is. That whole little ..." He screws up his face. "That group of them. And people your age, always looking to try and be different."

"I like the idea," Mom says suddenly. "If you two want to work on a business plan for how it could happen—"

I hurry to lift my hands. "Not me. Piper. Sorry, but I'm only at the diner for as long as I can, umm ..." My heart is pounding in my ears. This is the first part of the plan. The thing that is going to get me that much closer to living the life I want to live. "I'm opening a gym. Hopefully. I have some money saved up, and I'm going to start looking into it. Piper will be the one who gets the diner, and I'm okay with that."

To say Piper looks shocked to hell is an understatement. We've always known the place would be split between the two of us, but she loves it there. She actually enjoys going to work.

"Sorry," I say. "Probably should have talked to you first."

"Sorry? That's amazing. Are you serious?"

"Definitely. I want to use my degree. And Leon mentioned the town could use a gym, rather than people running over to Port Welling all the time. So I figured I might as well."

There's a beat of silence before Mom smiles. "That sounds like an excellent idea."

"Just"—Dad runs a hand over his mouth—"seems an unstable sort of business. The diner's solid, people need food. Who needs exercise?"

"Literally everyone." I barely manage to hold my smile back.

"Interesting." Grandpa turns to me, and the tone sets me on edge. "You're opening a gym, because Leon told you to. You're suggesting vegetarian foods for I'm assuming Kelly Atkins—and that pizza you and your gran made a while back was for him too, wasn't it?"

He might be old, but there's no denying he still has all his marbles. His tone is way too careful for me to relax. "It was."

He huffs a short, humorless thing. "Seems like

you've been hanging out with these gay boys a bit too much, Rowan. Eric Fletcher mentioned he sees you at the bar with that group sometimes."

"What does that have to do with anything?" I ask, forcing my tone to stay light, even though by this point I want to growl. I clench my hands under the table to stop anyone from seeing that they're shaking.

"You need to be careful. Be friends all you want, but those kids are sinners, and the last thing you want is to get messed up in that nonsense."

Nonsense? I lean forward and meet his stare. "You might need to spell that out for me."

"You know what I mean."

"Oh, do I?"

"They've lost their way, Rowan. Turned their backs on God and the church, and now they're doing devil knows what with their lives."

"You mean becoming a firefighter? Or running successful businesses?" My voice is growing loud. "Or finding loving relationships, or helping people out with whatever they need in town, or being kind and friendly and—"

His hand thumps down on the table. "This is what I mean. Walking out on church, the back talk and disrespect—"

"It's not disrespectful to point out when you're talking shit."

He splutters. "The *cursing*! What is going on with

you lately? You had your poor mother worried to death when you picked up and left and didn't bother to tell anyone." His eyes narrow. "Where have you been?"

"In LA."

His mouth gapes open for a second. "*With?*"

I could lie. It's not like they'd ever be able to verify the story, but the blood pumping thick in my ears is making it hard to think. It's urging me to be reckless. "With Circus."

"I knew it." He pushes his plate away. "I'm warning you, Rowan. That boy is trying to turn you into a fucking queer!"

My mouth drops as I stare at him. Then at Grandma, who's watching her plate, trying to block us out. Dad's looking at me in shock, and Mom's biting her lip.

Piper reaches for me, and when I meet her watery eyes, I know she knows. "Oh, Rowan ..."

And ... wait. It's not her eyes that are watery. It's her whole form.

I swallow thickly.

Then stand. "It'd be a bit hard for him to turn me when I've been *a fucking queer* all my life."

I toss my fork at my plate, and it rings out so loudly I almost miss the gasp. Someone sobs. But I can't tell who because I'm already tearing blindly from the room in a mad race to get to my room before anyone follows me.

I blink and blink again, trying to clear my vision as I grab my wallet and keys and those Polaroids and shove whatever else I need into my backpack before slinging it over my shoulder and racing for the door.

Piper beats me to it. Her eyes are big, cheeks streaked with tears. She steps forward without a word and gives me a tight hug.

"I'm so sorry," she whispers, just as Grandpa shouts, followed by the sounds of breaking china.

Piper darts away, and I leave.

Under no illusions about ever coming back.

FAKE FRIENDS

CHAPTER TWENTY SEVEN
CIRCUS

The tear of wheels through gravel echoes in the quiet house. It sets me on edge. Only Leon and Rowan know where I live, and Leon was having an early night tonight.

Rowan ... Well, I'd assumed he was going to have some quiet time at home.

But if it's not him, it's some random person at my house at night, and I'd prefer not to get murdered just when I'm starting to make plans. I mean, I had basically no future a month ago—couldn't a potential murder have been scheduled for then?

I cautiously approach the front door, wondering if I should have consulted the 8-Ball. Too late now.

Footsteps are coming down the front entrance, and it's only just now occurring to me that some kind of peephole probably would have been a good investment.

I jump as someone knocks heavily on the door.

"Circus!"

Oh, thank God.

"Circus!"

I scramble to unlock the door, and my smile splits my face when I open it to see Rowan standing there.

And then I take in his expression.

"Holy shit, are you okay?"

He drops his bag with a thump, then steps forward and pulls me in for a hug. He grips me hard, and I'm shocked into silence.

What the hell is going on?

Rowan's face presses into my neck, and his shoulders start to shake with quiet sobs. Whatever this is, it isn't good.

The bag, the crying.

Ohhh holy no …

Did they find out?

Because I'm an incredibly smart human, it's only just now hitting me how stupid those photos were. I bet they've seen them. And if they saw them and disowned him because of it …

I wrap my arms around him tighter and shift us away from the door. I kick it closed, turn the lock, and then sink into the hug.

If all of this is because of me, there's no way we'll be able to get past it.

Rowan's crying starts to calm.

"Do you want to talk about it or get drunk?"

He sighs against my shoulder and pulls away, revealing red eyes. "Can we fuck instead?"

I laugh. "I've created a monster."

That doesn't stop him from taking my hand and dragging me into my bedroom.

"Are you sure about this?" The speed he's undressing in has me worried.

"Completely. Now strip."

"I feel like you're deflecting emotion or some shit ..."

Rowan pauses, left only in his boxer briefs, and stalks toward me. His fingers are gentle as he reaches for my shirt and pulls it over my head. "We'll talk after." His lips skim my jaw. "Right now, I just want to get lost in you."

I tweak his nipple. "Are you calling me loose?"

His smile is fast but there, and it gives me a little hope. "You're perfect."

Well then. With sweet talking like that, he can get as lost as he likes.

He kisses me hard, and it's the most confident he's ever seemed as he strips me and walks me backward toward the bed.

Rowan breaks away from me long enough to get a condom and lube, and then he's back on me. And whatever's come over him, I don't hate it. He works me open with his fingers, and when he finally slides inside my body, I know what he means about getting lost.

He consumes me. His kisses, his rough hands, and with every rock of his hips he pegs my prostate, grinding as deep as he can manage.

"This, this is what I need," he pants.

His glazed eyes open and meet mine. I've always hated eye contact during sex, but for some reason, whenever Rowan does it, I can't look away.

He's so open and vulnerable.

I want him always.

His thrusting picks up, and I hurry to grab my cock to give it some relief. It only takes a few quick jerks before I'm spilling over my hand, and Rowan's not far behind me. He collapses on top of me in a sweaty, panting heap, and I reach up to run my fingers through his hair as I try to catch my breath.

He doesn't seem to be crying again which is an improvement.

Rowan pulls out and ditches the condom, but when I expect him to cuddle back in close to me, he settles against the headboard instead.

I reach for a shirt to wipe off my hand and stomach, then clean up the lube from my ass as best as I can. That shirt is headed for the trash.

By the time I crawl up next to him, Rowan's resting his head in his hands, and all the confidence he had during sex has completely disappeared.

I kiss his hair. "Ready to talk yet?"

"Talking is the last thing I want to do."

"Yep. I got that impression." I try for comforting. "Want to do it anyway?"

When he looks up again, the eyes that had been so full of lust a moment ago look sad. "I came out. To my family."

"Holy shit ..." Probably not the most supportive

response, but what does he expect? I'm legitimately in shock. "I have so many questions."

"Basically, Grandpa was going on with his shit and said you were trying to turn me gay. I said there's no way for you to turn me when I've been gay my whole life. And that's pretty much the whole story."

My heart is beating faster. "You mean … you didn't have to? You … you came out on purpose?"

His forehead wrinkles up. "Sort of? I guess. It's more that I was so mad and so tired of everything he was saying that I lost my mind over it."

He doesn't get it. Maybe he was angry or tired or whatever, but it doesn't matter what emotion was behind it because he said the words. And he meant to. "How many times has he said all those same things?"

Rowan shrugs. "I don't know. Hundreds."

"And did you ever come out before now?"

"Well, no, obviously."

"Exactly." I lick my lips and lean in a little so he's paying attention. "You were ready. And I'm so proud of you."

"I couldn't let him talk shit about you. I just couldn't."

"You did last time," I point out. Not to make him feel bad, but because I want him to know this was all him. I'm almost too scared to ask the next question. "What happened then?"

"I bolted. The last thing I wanted was to stick

around there and have them tell me how they really felt."

I doubt it's what I would have done, but who the hell am I to know? I never had to deal with the whole coming out thing. My mom always assumed I was straight until Rowan started coming around, *always*, and Dad picked up on it. Then they sat me down and told me they approved.

They didn't even give me a chance to go through all that emotional angst.

So what Rowan's going through ... I'm the last person who can give advice.

The fact he didn't stay and face them though, it makes me hope that maybe they won't all react the way he thinks they will.

"I'm glad you knew you could come to me," I finally say, reaching for his hand and linking our fingers together.

He tries to smile. "Not like I had anywhere else to go."

"Wow. Way to make a boy feel special."

That gets a laugh, even if it's a weak one. His thumb runs over the back of my hand. "You, umm, are, you know."

"What?"

"Special." Rowan pins me with his stare. "Especially to me."

His words make me unsettled, cloaking me in a completely foreign warmth that no one but him has ever made me feel before.

"It's been a long time since I've been special to anyone."

"What?" He turns to look at me. "What about your friends? And I swear everyone in town just lights up when you talk to them."

"It's cute you think that."

"Because it's true."

I press my lips against a smile. Tonight is not a happy kind of night, but when he says things like that, how am I supposed to react? "Well, I also think the same about you."

"At least we've got each other."

"Nope." I wriggle closer. "None of that. We're not going to be one of those couples who are completely reliant on each other. Tonight, we're going to sulk and curse the world, but tomorrow you need to reach out to your sisters at least."

He sighs. "I'll call Leita. At least I think she'll be okay. God—" He rubs his forehead. "I don't think I could survive if I never saw my nephews again."

"That won't happen." I squeeze his hand tighter, hoping I'm not just talking out of my ass. "And Piper?"

"Yeah, I don't know. But I guess this thing just happens one day at a time."

"Exactly."

He lets out a long breath as he hangs his head back. "I feel so sick."

"Yeah, I'm sorry."

"Don't be. Because I'm kind of relieved as well. There's no hiding anymore, and if I know my mom, she'll already be on the phone talking about it so ... yeah. I guess it's done."

Unfortunately, he's probably right about that. Lori Taylor, Joan Everett, and Brenda Harvey are like the town criers when it comes to spreading news.

I reach over and trace the tattoos on Rowan's hand. Nerves settle in my gut as I consider what I'm about to offer. "You can probably, you know, pick a bedroom or something while you're here. Not tonight though—I want you in here. I just mean if you have nowhere else to stay and you wanted to, like, move in, but not in a *moving in together* kind of way ..." That thought needs to immediately stop before I sound like even more of an idiot. "Sorry, rambling."

He chuckles. "It's cute. You're not usually a rambler."

"I don't usually ask my boyfriend to move in with me though either."

He doesn't immediately respond, and when I look up, his eyes have gone all wide.

It hits me.

Oh no, I dropped the *b* word. Well freaking done, Circus, you damn animal.

"I didn't mean—"

"I think I'm in love with you."

Now it's my turn to look like I've been hit in the face with a frying pan. "You … what?"

He nods. "I love you. And I want that."

I'm still in shock. "To … move in, or …?"

"To move in, like, in a separate room, of course. And to be boyfriends."

"Not roommates?"

He shakes his head. "Some dumb idiot told me roommates never works."

"He sounds wise." I push up and climb over Rowan's lap so I'm straddling him. "Do you mean it?"

"Yes."

"And you love me?"

He goes to look away, but I quickly grab his face. "Yes."

"Good. Because I love you too. And this time, there's no running away."

FAKE FRIENDS

CHAPTER TWENTY EIGHT
ROWAN

The buzz of my phone comes entirely too early for my liking. I blink open my eyes, and the first thing I see is Circus's naked form stretched out beside me. Everything that happened last night comes rushing back.

I still feel sick, of course, but I wasn't lying when I said there was relief there too.

With a quiet groan, I roll toward the side table and retrieve my phone.

Piper: *Are you okay?*

Circus is snoring quietly, and I'm growing to love that sound. But instead of pulling him close, like armor, I climb out of bed, pull on some underwear, and head for the opposite side of the house.

It's sort of surreal waking up here. The house is luxurious and not what I'm used to for sure, but it also feels right. Circus built this place for his future family, and hey, maybe one day that'll be me.

I start up his coffee maker once I get into the kitchen, then snap a photo in front of the same view

Circus is always posting. It's weird thinking that a few months back, I was looking at his photo in the exact same spot, wondering whether I should say good morning like the countless other people were.

Now I get to say it in person.

I post the photo, then open Piper's message again.

I finally text back.

Rowan: *I really don't know*
Piper: *Yikes*
Rowan: *Yup.*
Piper: *I'm so sorry. I didn't know.*
Rowan: *Of course you didn't. I kept it to myself as much as I could.*

I pour myself a cup of coffee and take a sip, needing the caffeine before I get into the rest of the conversation.

Rowan: *How were things after I left?*
Piper: *Umm ... tense. Which you'd probably guess.*
Rowan: *Yeah, I figured. Do I want to know what was said?*
Piper: *Not really. It was mostly Grandpa, if I'm honest. I don't think Gran said anything at all, and Mom and Dad were just ... I don't even know.*

That doesn't make me feel any better. At all.

Rowan: *Anyone even try to stand up for me?*
Piper: *By 'anyone' do you mean me?*
Rowan: *You'd fall under the umbrella of anyone, wouldn't you?*

It takes her a while to reply.

Piper: *I feel like shit that I didn't, if that's worth anything. He just wouldn't shut up—you know what he's like. I ended up just walking out. I'm sorry.*
Rowan: *I know you are.*

I can't accept her apology, but I *do* know what it's like. Once Grandpa gets started, no one stands a chance, not even Dad. I've seen them come to blows twice in semi-recent memory—the first time over Leita not working at the diner, and the second about me moving away for college—and those arguments had been so explosive, I really worried they were going to attack each other.

Apparently, accepting my sexuality wasn't as important as either of those things to my dad.

Warm arms circle my waist as Circus presses a kiss to my shoulder. "Good morning, boyfriend."

The word makes me all tingly. "Boyfriend."

"You like that?"

"So much." I pull him around so I can kiss him, not giving a shit about the morning breath situation we have going on. If I can wake up like this for the rest of my life, all the rest might actually be worth it.

He detangles himself from me to pour his own coffee, and I reluctantly let him go. "Plans today?"

"Hide?"

Circus cracks a warm smile. "Solid plan. While we do that, I was thinking we could talk some more about your gym idea."

"What about it?"

"Come on." Circus grabs my hand with the one not holding his coffee. He leads me to his studio and through to another little room I've never seen before.

On his desk, he has a pad covered in scribbled numbers.

"What's all this?"

He clicks his computer and shows me a spreadsheet. "This is what we need to do in order to start up a business. This is some of the equipment I worked out you'd need, along with rent, utilities …"

He wasn't joking when he said he'd been planning.

I point to an address at the top. "This is just down from Harvey's."

"Yep. It's where I normally display my art for all the festivals, but since it sits empty for the rest of the year, I thought you'd put it to better use than me. We can have the names changed over."

"But what would you use?"

Circus shrugs. "I have a bunch of options up my

sleeve. None of which need a physical space."

I'm overwhelmed. I have no idea what to say to him, because I'm not positive about how I feel. I'd assumed I'd be left to do all of this on my own, but Circus has done the bulk of the work in one afternoon. When I'd talked about opening a gym, I'd assumed it would be a year or so away.

Then again, I have no idea if I'm even welcome at Harvey's, and without the diner, I'm technically unemployed.

Something I've never been in my life.

I know Circus won't want rent from me, but I refuse to be a freeloader either. So opening the gym as quickly as possible will stop me burning through the money I made with Circus.

He turns to me, and something in my expression makes his face drop. "Did I overstep? Shit, I did, right? Sorry. I'm not exactly seasoned when it comes to relationships."

And hearing his uncertainty is the thing that makes me sure. I smile and pull him in for a hug.

"This is perfect. You're perfect. And you're an idiot if you think I'm ever letting you go."

He presses his face to my shoulder and laughs. "That might be the creepiest thing you've ever said to me."

"Wait until I tell you I want to wear you like a hat."

"Hmm …" Circus pulls back. "That sounds promising actually." He grabs my hand again and drags me after him.

"Where are we going?"

"The bedroom. I want to test that out."

Chapter Twenty Nine
Circus

I'm actually doing it. Having a real-life human boyfriend move in with me. This is the whole reason for my house, exactly what I had planned, and now it's happening I'm just waiting for everything to fall apart.

Rowan being here when I woke up, and after my morning hike, and using the shower in the afternoon before he came out smelling like my body wash and wearing soft sweatpants ...

I'm tempted to snap a picture of him to post, knowing it would rack up the interactions, but something holds me back.

The damp hair, the dark ink, his tight muscles ... all mine. Now I know why he stopped me from posting those Polaroids. There's something almost possessive about my want to keep him to myself.

I mean, the world has seen him practically naked, but that was staged. For some reason this feels different.

This moment, right here, all mine.

And that's sort of fucking terrifying.

What would Mom and Dad say if they could see me now?

They'd liked Rowan; Mom had felt bad for him. But if they had known he was the one who'd punched me, would they have been as forgiving as I was?

My conscience keeps telling me I shouldn't have given in so easily, but I was tired of holding on to that. Besides, I wanted to forgive him. I have for years.

Obviously the first chance I got I was going to give in.

But I never for a minute thought we'd end up dating.

We hole up at my place for two days, planning Rowan's gym. The purpose helps take his mind off his family and what they currently think of him.

I wish I could tell them all how amazing he is.

I climb onto the couch where Rowan is sitting and slide into his lap. His face is immediately taken over with a grin that makes me smile in return, and I link my hands behind his neck.

"Want to head down and look at the shop today? I can invite Leon so you can make a plan with him."

"Leon?"

"Well, you're going to need to convert the space to a gym, and Leon's the best."

"Sounds good." He pulls me in for a kiss. "How about you blow me and we'll go?"

Yep. This whole having a boyfriend for a roommate thing is working out nicely. I sink to my knees, finish him off, and then we're both ready to head out.

We take his car since he actually likes to drive, and I

make a mental note to buy him a bike. In weather like this, there's nothing better than being outside and enjoying it.

Leon texts me on the way to say he's at the diner and he'll meet us in ten.

Perfect.

The storefront I lease is a large, bare space. That worked for me because technically all I needed were walls and space to set up easels, but if it's going to be an actual gym, it's going to need a lot of work done to it.

"Just over here." I point to the corner of O'Connell Road and Juniper Lane.

"I remember." Rowan shoots me a cocked eyebrow, and I cringe. During the Sunflora Festival he'd tried to talk to me, and I'd told him to fuck off and literally locked the doors in his face.

"I mean, I never claimed to be mature," I say.

"No one would believe you if you did."

I laugh and follow him from the car to the store and unlock the doors.

It's dim and empty, and I can't work out if the lack of furniture makes it look smaller or bigger than it is.

Rowan nods. "Change rooms could work back there."

"A front desk here?"

"Maybe an office in this corner where I can store stuff, and that whole back wall could be mirrored."

"There's nothing hot and sweaty people love more

than a mirror."

"Speaking from experience?"

"We'll give it a test drive before opening day."

The words have barely left my mouth when a throat clears behind me. "I walked in at the wrong time."

"Or the right one." I turn a grin on Leon. "The whole time you're in here building, you can picture what we'll be getting up to when you're done."

"That is actually the last thing I want to be picturing. Ever. Let alone while I'm working."

"So you'll take the job?"

His forehead creases as he looks around the space. "Run me through what you want first."

And he can act as reluctant as he likes, as soon as he and Rowan start making plans, I can tell he's invested. Leon is a builder by trade, but it's because it's what he *loves* doing. Creating shit with his hands, getting dirty and sweaty.

I'll never understand the appeal.

But it's real work. And it gives him purpose.

I used to think what I did gave me purpose too. All the interactions, the fans, they were the ones breathing life into my existence.

The thing is though, since Rowan moved in, I've posted once and that was only because he suggested it. I'm not constantly monitoring my comments and messages, and while I watch him and Leon chat through the plans, pulling out my phone and taking a picture is so far down my list of needs I'm struggling to remember what was so important about it all.

If I'm not taking and posting photos though, what *am* I going to do with my time?

I've worked hard for years, trying to build a name and brand for myself, and I do enjoy it most of the time.

But it's also a lot of pressure to make sure I post consistently and think of different shots and themes. In the scheme of things, it's nothing compared to what Tanner and Leon are doing, but literally the only thing that keeps me going is my passion for it.

If that's gone, what then?

I love that Rowan is here, putting plans in place to start a business he's passionate about. I'll help him of course, but this is his thing, and when it comes to personal training and exercise, I couldn't think of anything I'd rather be doing less.

But I also can't think of anything I'd rather be doing more either.

I have no clue where *I* go from here.

FAKE FRIENDS

CHAPTER THIRTY
ROWAN

I couldn't believe it when Leita messaged and invited both me and Circus over. I'm not getting my hopes up, but the fact she didn't ask me to come solo can only be a good sign.

Right?

Jesus, I don't know. This whole thing has had my stress levels at ten, and every time I imagine this catch-up going well, I picture at least ten more scenarios where it doesn't.

We walk side by side up the garden path toward the front door. There's a lot of noise coming from inside, and I'm pretty sure my nephews must be overthrowing a continent with all the yelling going on. It makes my heart hurt, trying to imagine not seeing their faces anymore. I've already missed out on way too much time in their lives.

"Hey, guys," Laurie says as he meets us at the front door. "Leita's just putting some snacks together." He shakes my hand, then Circus's, and there's no hint of anything wary about him. Another good sign.

"Uncle Ro!" Jase collides with my side like the little

tornado he is. "Can you come help me with Mario Kart? Levi never lets me win."

I laugh. "Not right now, buddy. But let me talk to your mom and I will."

He runs off with a "Levi, you're in trouble now!"

God, those kids melt my heart. When I look over at Circus, he's wearing the same dicky smile as I am, but his is directed my way. "What?"

"Nothing at all."

Uh-huh.

This whole thing is so much easier with him by my side.

We reach the kitchen, and Laurie takes a seat at the counter just as Leita pulls a tray of mini quiches out of the oven.

"Rowan, Circus, hey. Do you want coffee? Something stronger?"

"I'll make it." I hurry into the kitchen, but Leita gently pushes me out again.

"I like looking after my guests. Now sit your ass down."

I'm certainly not going to argue with her. Circus has already grabbed a stool, so I quickly slip onto the one between him and Laurie.

"So you guys are dating?" Leita finally asks once she's finished making drinks for us all.

It's on the tip of my tongue to deny it, total reflex, but Circus grabs my hand resting on the counter and answers for me.

"We are. And if it wasn't for your parents, we probably would have started a long time ago."

She hums, watching me. "Were you together in high school?"

That one I can deny. "No. I wanted to be, but ... I was too messed up."

"So what changed?"

"I tried to date women in Portland, but it never went anywhere. Then I saw a psychiatrist and basically worked through a lot of the lies I'd been telling myself for years. It's still hard, but it's not possible to walk away from Circus again. I love him."

Leita smiles at that. "I did always wonder. I mean, I didn't really think you were together or anything, but you were closer with Circus than your other friends. You always came home smiling whenever you'd been with him."

I had no idea I'd been that obvious. Oops?

"And then when you started hanging out again, and you were hardly around—"

"I was here every week to babysit."

She laughs. "I know, I'm not saying you disappeared. But Mom and Dad mentioned you must have been seeing someone because you were being quiet about who you were spending your days off with. I'm not sure I jumped right to *that* conclusion, but I figured it was Circus you were with."

The fact she's just covered all that and doesn't look ready to throw me out of her house has the knots in my stomach ease. "Did you know? That I'm gay?"

"Nope. I figured you weren't as homophobic as the rest of them, but you hid it well."

She says it like a compliment, but I'm struggling to take it that way. "And you're okay with all this?"

"Why wouldn't I be?"

"Well, we had the same upbringing. And it was hard for me to accept myself—I don't know how it's so easy for you."

She reaches forward and takes my other hand. "I might like acting as some 1950s housewife. I might like being domestic and a mother and keeping my husband happy. But I'm also headstrong and capable of critical thinking. I'm smart, I educate myself, and I don't buy into the bullshit about queer people. I know you, Rowan, and no matter how much Grandpa wants to rant and curse about me letting you near the boys, I don't give a damn. You're always welcome here."

My whole body is hit with a burst of emotion so strong, I think I'm going to cry again. I hold it in though, because apparently Circus is the only one I'll treat to that fun sight. Lucky him. I thought the idea of Grandpa spreading his hate and trying to turn people against me would affect me more than it does though. After a lifetime of hearing it all before, I guess I don't expect anything else from him.

"I'd hate to get on your wrong side, Leita," Circus says, picking up one of the cookies she's set out and putting the whole thing in his mouth. "But now I'm dating your brother, we're basically family, yeah? That means you're always on my side, so I'm liking this decision of mine better and better."

She laughs. "Deal. Unless it's against my brother, then I'll be coming for you, dude."

"Sounds fair."

We spend the rest of the afternoon there, me fulfilling my promise to Jase to kick Levi's ass at Mario Kart. Laurie takes me outside to talk me through some renovation plans he and Leita are talking about, and Circus *tries*, and fails, to help Leita cook dinner.

I come back in to find him banished from the kitchen and playing with my nephews in the living room. He's swinging Blake around and causing my nephew to cackle uncontrollably.

Circus's smile is enormous when he catches sight of me. "Goddamn, I love kids."

"Yeah, they're pretty great." I watch him for a moment. "You said you wanted your own, right?"

"I do. It doesn't have to be soon or anything, but it's one hundred percent on the cards for me. One day. Until then ..." He blows a raspberry on Blake's foot. "I have your nephews to entertain."

I've never heard of anything more perfect.

FAKE FRIENDS

Chapter Thirty One
Circus

After the day at Leita's, Rowan somehow becomes even more affectionate. I didn't know that was possible, but I do know I love it. He doesn't shy away from me when we go into town, and his entire online presence is photos of the two of us.

The only dark spot hanging over our heads is the fact his parents still haven't made contact. Assholes.

"Holy shit," Rowan says, and he angles his phone so I can see the message.

And like I've summoned them from thought alone, I read Piper's message.

Mom and Dad want to meet you at the diner. Can you come? Please?

"Shit is right," I mutter. "What are you going to do?"

Rowan lets out a long exhale. "I don't know. I mean, I think I want to go."

"Really? After how they've treated you?"

I watch him chew on his lip for a moment. "If I don't, I'll keep wondering. They're my parents, you know? I want things to be good with them, but I'm also annoyed they didn't bother to message me themselves."

"Yeah, that's low."

"I don't know, Circus." He rubs a hand over his face. "I know what I went through, and aren't they just dealing with the same thing?"

"Nope." Fuck that. I'm not letting Rowan compare his struggles with their closed-mindedness. "I think you should go. Not for them, for you. And if they're assholes, we'll tell them where to stick it."

"You'd come with me?"

"Of course." I'm sort of offended he even needs to ask.

"You have no idea how much that means to me."

I do though. I know Rowan better than anyone.

"But I think I should do this on my own."

"Okay." I'm not going to fight him over spending time with his family. They're not top of my list. "Why?"

"First, I think it'll be easier on them if I'm not shoving us in their faces—"

"You want to make it easier on *them*?"

"Only initially. But also, my sexuality isn't tied to you. I don't want them thinking that all it will take for me to be straight is for us to break up. I want to face them, as a gay man, and try to make them understand."

I lean forward and pinch his chin. "You're amazing, and I love you."

"You too." He smiles and ducks down to kiss my

fingers. "I have to do whatever I can to make it right with them."

I'm nervous the whole time he spends getting ready, feeling out of my skin with worry. I can't shake the feeling that something is going to go wrong.

His family is important to him, I get that. I also know I'm important to him.

But if they ask him to give me up ... I'm still not sold on how that ends.

Rowan leaves me with a kiss, and I do my best not to let my worry show. I'm just going to keep faking confidence for him and hoping everything's okay.

Until I watch his car pull away and close my door.

My phone starts to ring.

Preston's name is on the display.

Huh, maybe this is where my bad feeling was coming from, because I'm willing to put money down that he's going to yell at me for my lack of presence lately.

"I'm alive and happy, thanks for asking," I say before he has a chance to get started.

To my surprise, he actually manages a laugh. "What a surprise, me too."

I scrunch up my face as I make my way back into my living area. "That can't be right. You're talking to me."

"Exactly! And why wouldn't I be happy to talk with my current favorite client?"

"Have you been drinking? You're drunk, right?"

He laughs *again*, and again I'm not sure what's gotten into him. Preston has always been an okay guy—it's one of the reasons I hired him—but *jovial*? Nope. It's not a trait he's known for.

"I haven't been drinking yet. But I have a feeling once this conversation is over, we're both going to have a lot to celebrate."

That gets my attention. I push off the wall I'm leaning against and transfer my phone to the other ear. "I'm listening."

"Start packing your bags, Circus. I'm looking at a contract for your first movie role."

My jaw hits the ground, and I barely pick it up in time to say, "You've got to be shitting me."

"Not at all. There's an audition clause obviously, but that's more of a formality. They want you. And they're paying a lot."

I shake my head. "You know I don't give a shit about money. What's the movie about? Big studio or indie?"

"*Big* studio. There's some names being thrown around for your costar too, and the best part for you is that it's a romance with two male leads."

"That *is* amazing." Excitement is starting to bubble in my gut. "I'm … it sounds perfect."

"Even better, I told them your character *has* to be pan, and that needs to be in the script somewhere. They want you so badly, they immediately agreed."

And even though I'm excited, I'm also savvy enough

to know this is unusual. "Why me though?"

"The studio won't be giving this movie a huge budget, by Hollywood standards, anyway. But the producers have been told if it does well, they'll be free to create more queer content. You have a platform. And you've done acting classes, which is more than some of the other influencers they were looking at. They have money and great writers. What they need is people who can market this thing to death."

"I'm so in." My smile is hurting my face, and I cannot wait to share my news with Rowan. Everything is falling so perfectly into place I can barely believe it.

"Good. Because after this, you won't be social famous anymore, Circus. You'll be *actual* famous."

Which is everything I've ever worked toward. But …

With something like that, my life will change. Just when I'm at a point that I can enjoy myself now.

Still, this isn't an opportunity I can pass up.

"Filming starts in about two months, which is a good amount of time for you to wind down the pretend love with Rowan. Make it sound like an amicable separation, of course."

It takes an embarrassingly long time for the words to sink in. "Separate? From Rowan?"

"Of course. That relationship has done what it needed to, and once you're on set in Greece, we'll start orchestrating your friendship with your costar. The producers don't want to push the *dating* thing, but they do want people questioning how close you two are, and we don't need some fake boyfriend getting in the way of that."

Break up? Filming in Greece?

"Umm ... I don't want to break up."

"Well, it'll be a poor look to seem like you're cheating on your boyfriend. What's the problem? He's got a platform now, and you're getting everything you've worked toward for years."

Years. And that's the thing.

Everything with Rowan is great for *right now*, but I've been pushing for this since I started my site. Giving it all up because I have a sliver of happiness, a hint at the family I've always wanted, is ridiculous.

All it would take is Rowan to decide he's done with me, and then I'm left with nothing again. No real boyfriend, no fake boyfriend, no movie contract.

If I don't take this, I'm not dumb enough to think anything else will come along. This is it.

Preston must take my silence for the stunned variety, rather than the holy-shit-my-whole-life-is-resting-on-this-moment type, because he chuckles.

"I'll send over the contract and the script. Go celebrate."

I hang up without saying goodbye.

Chapter Thirty Two
Rowan

When it comes to my family, I've always been okay with them having the upper hand. I let them talk at me, I never complain or back-talk. I'm respectful to a fault, but that was mostly because I didn't want them to ever guess about this other side of me that I've worked for so long to keep hidden.

Well, it's out there now.

So as I walk into the diner, I keep my head high even though I'm preparing for a full-frontal assault.

I don't know if it'll just be Piper there, or the whole Harvey clan, but I do know that I'm ready for a fight if it comes to it.

The thing I'm not sure about is whether Circus will be there for me when it's over.

He's seemed so in this thing since I showed up the other night, but the last thing I want is for being in a relationship with me to make things hard for him.

I need to confront my family and let them know nothing is going to change and if they don't like it, fine. But they're to keep away from Circus.

I'm all but holding my breath when I finally get to

Harvey's Burger Bar and push through the door.

The tinkle of the bell overhead is familiar in a soul-deep way. And even though I don't want to keep working here, it would kill me to never step foot back in the place.

I glance around at the usual regulars, smiling at a few of them, and then make my way over to where Piper is manning the coffee machine.

There's a part-timer out back working the grill, and thankfully I don't see any other family around.

"What's good here?" I ask, sliding into the stool closest to my sister. She immediately spins at my voice, and her face breaks into a smile.

"It's about time. Where have you been?"

Truthfully? "Hiding."

"Still with Circus?"

"Well, he's my boyfriend, so …"

Piper crosses her arms and leans on the counter. "Boyfriend? Wow. Congratulations."

"Yeah. Thanks."

She's smiling, but I can't quite read how she feels. It's definitely off compared to what she's normally like, but I don't think it's completely bad. "Are we okay?"

"Of course." She hurries to squeeze my arm. "Yes, totally. I am one hundred percent happy for you."

"Then what's with the face?"

"I'm sorry. I swear it's not you. Really. I'm just struggling with the being single thing right now. And while I'm happy for you, like, legitimately *thrilled*, it's also reminding me I'm still alone."

Well, thank God for that. "Piper, you're one of the best people I know. But ... maybe you need to let Tanner go already. I'm well aware of how hypocritical that sounds coming from me when I've never been able to forget Circus, but him and Royce ... I dunno. I can't see that ever ending."

"Yeah, I know." She wipes over the counter. "They were always sort of inevitable, weren't they?"

I'd like to think Circus and I were too.

The bell above the door sounds again, and I glance back over my shoulder to see Mom and Dad walk in ... with Father O'Connor. This does *not* seem promising.

"Rowan, thank the Lord," Mom says, hurrying over.

"Yeah, hi."

"I didn't know if you'd come." She almost sounds ... worried. I try not to let it get my hopes up.

"I didn't know if I wanted to."

"And now?"

My gaze flicks toward Father O'Connor and Dad as they slide into a booth in the corner. "Undecided."

"Where have you been staying?"

"With Circus ..."

Her inhale is sharp. "I thought you might say that. Rowan ..."

"Are—are you mad?"

"No. No, no, no. I'm ..." She lets out a watery sniff. "I love you." It sounds more like she's trying to convince herself than remind me. "We just want to have a conversation. Talk through some things."

I'm uncomfortably aware of what those things might be. "Fine. Let's get it over with."

We join the booth with Dad and Father O'Connor, and as I slide in beside Mom and she takes my hand, a lump lodges itself in my chest. I'm itching to jump up and run out of here, but I need to stand my ground. Running won't change a damn thing.

"Thanks for meeting us," Dad says gruffly, staring at the table.

I don't bother responding.

Father O'Connor reaches a hand across the table. "Rowan, good to see you again."

"You too." I give it a solid shake. "Sorry, I'm just struggling to work out what you're doing here for a family conversation."

"While I'm a priest, I also have experience with family reconciliations. Your parents asked me here to provide support for you all."

Support for us *all* or just *them*?

"Who would like to start?" Father O'Connor asks.

"I think we just need more information, Rowan," Mom says. "I mean, how long have you been ...?"

"Gay? Forever. It's not something that just happens."

"No, of course not ..."

"You're disappointed."

"Rowan ... I could never be disappointed. I'm, well, worried. We're *all*"—she gestures to Dad—"worried."

"I bet some of you are more than worried."

"That's not fair."

"Isn't it? Dad? Are you seriously going to say you and Grandpa haven't already disowned me?"

He takes a measured breath. "I won't disown you. I'm just struggling to understand."

"What is so hard to understand?"

"You played football, and had that nice girlfriend, and—"

"What he means is, it's just not something we were prepared for," Mom says. "You took us all by surprise, and now I have a beautiful son who's all these things that we've been told are sinful, and Rowan, I just, I don't know. I *know* you're good, and I'll always love you, but I'm ... struggling. I mean ... are you *sure* you're gay? Maybe you just haven't found the right—"

"*Don't*. I know what you're going to say, and it'll just piss me off." I want to get angry and tell her to fuck off, but what she's going through now is the same thing I've struggled with since I first realized that I didn't look at girls the way my friends did. "I know," I finally say. "I've had the same little voice, all my life, telling myself I'm wrong, or disgusting. And I've *tried* to fight this, Mom. So much. But I couldn't." Tears are pushing at the backs of my eyes, but I refuse to let them out this time.

Dad lets out a heavy breath. "We have a deal for

you."

I don't like the sound of that. I glance over to where Leon's just walked in and send him the best *help* eyes I possibly can, but he just turns and walks out again.

"We'll accept this ... *thing*, on one condition."

"Which is?" I eye him warily, knowing I'm not going to like what he's about to say.

"We want you to get help. Ah, therapy, if you will. Father O'Connor knows of a good place with good people."

"Conversion therapy?" I reel back from the thought of it. Yes, I might have considered it years ago, but I know better now.

"Strictly voluntary," Father O'Connor says, raising his hands. "I know there are some bad places out there, but this one is all aboveboard. Nothing illegal. That said, it'll only work if you want it to work. I don't recommend it to anyone whose mind is set on homosexual ways."

I'm breathing heavier, gripping the table edge with one hand and squeezing Mom's tighter with the other. "You would rather I went through this and made myself unhappy than accept me as I am?"

"Come on, Rowan," Dad snaps. "The Bible is clear. You're our son, and we only want what's best for you." To my surprise and horror and shock, he blinks back tears. "We're scared. Scared that if you go down this path your soul will be ..." He can't even say the words. "We love you. And maybe this will help, maybe it won't, but all we're asking is that you try. If you try this for us, and it doesn't work, when you get back, it will be our turn. We'll accept you, and ... your *partner*."

He can't even say Circus's name. "And if I don't go?"

The despair on his face recedes. "Then this is it for us. Standing by while you do nothing would not make us responsible parents. If you won't even try and rid yourself of this thing, what do you expect us to do?"

Love me anyway?

The thing is, I understand though. I don't want to—I fucking *hate* that I do. But all these years I've been trying to deny myself have been directly linked to their exact same thought process. We're all so fucking brainwashed.

It's taken me years to get to a point where I finally want to accept who I am. How long is it going to take them?

If I don't do this, I'll lose them. Yes, Piper and Leita will still be here for me, but these are my *parents*.

What if I went? It'd be a few months at the most, then I'd come back and they'd have to hold up their end of the deal. By Christmas, everything could be exactly the way I've always wished it would be and never dared to actually believe.

But it would mean leaving Circus. Even for only a short time, it's the last thing I want to do.

But do I really have a choice?

FAKE FRIENDS

Chapter Thirty Three
Circus

My phone rings and I hurry to answer.

"I think you need to get down here now."

I frown at Leon's supposed greeting. "What are you talking about?"

"Rowan's at Harvey's, and he's sitting with his parents and Father O'Connor. He looked like he was shitting himself."

"The *priest*? Jules's dad?"

"Yup. Now get off your ass and come save your boyfriend."

My mouth actually falls open as I lower my phone from my ear and end the call.

What the *fuck* are his parents playing at?

Rowan said he was going to meet them, but he didn't mention anything about Father O'Connor. So either they've completely blindsided him with it, or … he kept it from me.

I'm kind of terrified of what that means, but I can't believe that Rowan is wanting back in the closet. He wouldn't. He *knows* that doesn't work.

But he said he wants to do this on his own.

My brain feels stuck as I make for my bedroom and fall face-first onto the bed.

This is too much.

Part of me wishes Leon hadn't called because the concern in his voice ... I bury my head under a pillow.

Rowan's gay. I know that. He knows that. And what we have is so electric, I don't want to let it go.

But would he?

Sure, I want to believe things are great, but with his family barely speaking to him ... will he work out that life with me will be a thousand times more complicated than the one he was pretending to live?

It's a harsh question maybe, but knowing what he's been through, it's a legitimate one.

And ...

Well, *can* he have a life with me?

This movie offer is the biggest opportunity I've ever had. It would be borderline certifiable for me to turn it down. *Especially* for Rowan who, at this point, could still be a total flight risk.

I want him. Hell, I fucking love him.

But is it enough?

If I turn down the movie and he leaves, it would leave me with no movie, no Rowan, and the followers I've built because of our relationship would slowly dwindle away.

I'd be back to having nothing.

Panic seizes me, and I hurry to sit up and breathe

through it. The bone-numbing loneliness is always lurking just beneath the surface, and even though Rowan has been a bandage for that, I'm terrified he'll rip the bandage away and I'll be left exposed. Alone.

This movie … I'd make more friends, expand my reach, potentially sign on for more of the same, and the more popular I get, the more certain it is I'll always have people around.

Always.

Just … not Rowan.

And he's the one I want.

The *only* one.

The awareness seeps through my desperate thoughts.

I moved away from people for a reason. I needed that barrier for protection while I built myself back up, but a family's the end goal. It's *always* been the end goal.

The thought of having that with Rowan actually lights me up inside.

It stills the panic in a way that nothing else does.

But it's a huge gamble.

I swallow and glance at my 8-Ball. It hasn't steered me wrong before.

I pick it up, the smooth surface heavy in my hand.

All I have to do is ask, *Should I fight for Rowan?*

Yes, and I'll kiss the movie goodbye. Yes, and I'll go down there and bail him out just like Leon wants me to do. To show Rowan that I'm there for him. Always.

And if it says no ... the panic simmers back to the surface. If it says no, I'll do the movie.

Leave.

I glance down at the little view screen to see a corner of the options bob pathetically into view.

I imagine the answer. Some version of *My reply is no* or *very doubtful* and then I ... leave.

I leave.

I *can't* leave.

The ball rolls out of my hand and hits the floor with a loud thud before rolling out of sight.

I can't do the movie.

I can't walk away from him.

No matter what, even if this is too much for him, I have to *try*.

And that trying starts with getting my ass back in the car and heading for the diner.

There's just enough time to switch out my T-shirt for one that doesn't stink of clammy indecision, and then I'm back in the car, tearing toward town.

I find a parking space a block away from the diner, and in my enthusiasm, the front of the bumper hits the gutter.

Oops?

I scramble out of the car, trying to both calm the fuck down and get there as quickly as I can. It's been at least twenty minutes since Leon called me, so I have no clue if they're still in there, but if they are ... yep. I'm ready.

Probably.

Until I get to the door.

Will I even be welcome inside? Rowan's whole family probably hates me if he told them about us, and I wouldn't put it past his dad to throw me out on my ass.

Nope, I'm doing this.

Just casually going to stake my claim in front of a diner of people who've known me my whole life.

Nothing to see here.

Fuck.

I push the door open.

They're the first ones I see.

Rowan looks panicked. All big eyes staring at the table. His dad isn't looking at him, and his mom seems to be trying to make up for it by looking at him *too* intently. Father O'Connor just looks plain sad.

And this kind of depressing shit is stopping right now.

The door opens behind me again and this time Leon, Royce, and Tanner walk in. Leon nods my way as they take over a booth, not bothering to hide the way they're staring. Just seeing them confirms to me that I've made the right choice.

Here I go, then. Sucking in a deep breath, I make my way over.

"Mr. and Mrs. Harvey. Father O'Connor. So good to see you all again." I grab Rowan's shoulder and give it a squeeze, ignoring the way I can feel him staring up at me. "I've gotta say, I'm disappointed I wasn't invited to lunch."

"Circus." Brenda manages a small smile even as her husband looks like he might be sick. "We're just having a family conversation."

"Perfect timing, then. I'm family, I'll join too." But just as I go to move away and find a chair, Rowan grabs me. He pushes closer to his mom and makes room for me beside him.

Even better.

Rowan's grip on my hand is tight. "What are you doing here?" he murmurs.

"Leon called me."

I feel some of the tension leave his body as he presses against my side.

"So what are we talking about?"

No one answers me at first. Then, Rowan's voice is soft as he says, "Conversion therapy."

Cold creeps through me. My voice turns brittle. "What?"

"It's a suggestion," Father O'Connor says.

My free hand slaps down on the table. "Are you people fucking shitting me?"

"Circus, this place isn't like those horror stories you read about—"

"Is it designed with the intent to turn queer people straight?"

"Well, that is the main—"

"Then yeah, it is just as bad." I swing around to Rowan's parents. "Do you have any clue how much your opinions have already fucked with Rowan's head? He's spent the last decade—at least—of his life trying to hide this side of himself, and now you're asking for *more*? What is wrong with you?"

"It's just a suggestion," Karl snaps. "We're not being unreasonable here. We care about him, and we need to see him at least try, and if that doesn't work—"

"Try?" My voice shakes dangerously, but I can't believe the words coming out of their mouths. "What do you think it was like for him in high school? With his friends pressuring him to date and knowing that if he dated *me* he'd probably never hear from his family again? Or the first time we finally kissed and he freaked out so badly he punched me in the face? Or the five years since that he's spent dating women and forcing himself through being with them even though they do literally nothing for him? You don't think that's *trying*?"

And maybe I'm speaking for Rowan here, but all I want to do is throw a giant fuck-you in all their faces.

"Don't you want what's best for him?" Brenda asks.

"Yeah, I do. So it's a no on the therapy. Because Rowan and I have spent too much time apart already, and if there's anything the past five years have taught us, it's that we're miserable if we're not together."

"You love him ..." she says slowly.

Rowan turns to her. "You know how you and Dad always tell us that when you first met, you just knew? There was never anyone else. That when you were together it was like someone had filled you with sunlight?"

"Yes ..."

"That's how I feel about Circus. How I've *always* felt."

"Wow. I—I don't know what to say."

Karl clears his throat and pointedly turns his attention to the rest of the room.

My hand in Rowan's seems to give him a boost.

"I've tried to be with women, for you guys, and it never made me happy. So if you still want me in your lives, it's your turn to try for me."

"Rowan ..."

"And tell Grandpa that means no backhanded comments, no insulting me or my boyfriend, and the rest of you need to forget everything you've been told about gay men and accept me the way I am."

"It's not that easy—"

"*I* know that. I've been dealing with it for most of my life. But either you support me, or ..." He hesitates, and I squeeze his hand to go on. "Or this is it for us."

After everything he's been through, I'm both proud and sad to hear the words. But they needed to be said.

Father O'Connor slides a shiny brochure across the table. "I think it would be a good idea to pause this conversation and have time to think all this through. Process where each side is coming from."

"Nope." I grab the brochure and scrunch it in my hand. "Thanks, Father, but Rowan was perfectly clear."

He nods, looking mildly disappointed. "You know where to find me. Both of you."

Rowan's dad follows him out of the booth. "We'll take some time to talk." He motions for Brenda to follow him, so Rowan and I quickly jump out to let her pass.

She pauses in front of her son and squeezes his arm. "I love you. No matter what."

"You too, Mom."

His dad doesn't say anything else as they leave.

Once the bell signals they've gone, I let out a long breath and crush Rowan in a hug. "Fuck me."

"Yeah."

We sink back into the booth, both of us drained from the whole conversation.

"You okay?"

"I guess. And as much as I love that you're here, I really wish you didn't have to see all that."

"Rowan, I'm here because I choose you. Because I want to be with you, and I want to try and start a life together. That means taking on your family as well."

"You've always been too good for me," he mutters.

"Eh, I'm just a messy person falling for an equally messy person." I lift his head so he's looking at me. "I love you."

"Thank God you still do." His eyes fall closed as he rests his forehead against mine. "You're sure I'm not too much—"

"Nope. And I never want you thinking that again." I look up as Leon pats my shoulder and slides in across from us, along with Royce and Tanner. Piper arrives a few minutes later with soda for everyone, and she squashes in next to me.

"Could have gone better?" Leon finally asks.

"Yeah, but it also could have been worse," Rowan says.

Piper leans forward to look at her brother. "They'll come around."

"I'm not so sure. But I guess we'll see."

I know he's trying to keep his hopes down, and while I think today was a dick thing for them to ask him, I can also see it for what it was. A way for them to try to hold on to their son.

"How does it feel?" Tanner asks. "To be finally out?"

"I still don't know. It feels good, and I keep getting these panicked moments that I'll wake up and realize I haven't actually done it yet, but I'd be lying if I said I wasn't worried about what people will think."

"Eh." I shrug. "You'd be brave enough to do it again. And again. And the thing is ... people around here have known us since we were kids. I have to believe the majority of them want us to be happy."

"Look at you, being all sentimental."

I give him a dry look, but he's right. Even after all that bullshit with his parents, even after letting the idea of the movie role go and putting all my hopes in this relationship, I'm not freaking out like I thought I would be.

The worry is gone, and all that's left is this deep contentment as I look around at the people sitting at this table.

I might not have a family in the traditional sense, but if today's taught me anything, I do have people who care about me. Leon, Royce, Tanner. The people in this town.

It's a good feeling.

And now, with Rowan, I no longer feel lost. This is where I'm meant to be.

FAKE FRIENDS

Chapter Thirty Four
Rowan

I stare down at the photo of Circus and me from a few minutes ago.

"Are you sure you want to do this?" he asks.

I almost laugh. Am I sure? Hell no. I'm about to put my entire life online for a bunch of strangers to pass judgment.

These posts aren't my life, not like Circus. I want them to know why I hid and why I won't be posting as frequently anymore.

If I lose all my followers today, it's not something I care about, but Circus has been working at this for years. It's important to him, even if there's an element to it that isn't healthy. It doesn't matter. If it's important to him, it's important to me too.

Except now I have no words. I mean, how do you sum up twenty-four years of gay-bashing yourself? How do I put into words that I hated who I am and wanted to stamp that out of me? That I'd considered conversion therapy and maybe would have gone through with it if it didn't require me to come out first.

There are so many elements, so many layers. And

the last thing I want is for any of it to come across like I'm making excuses. Too many people go through what I did, and they're not all lucky enough to have found a support system to help them through it.

Man, if I had never seen that psychologist in the first place, I might never have had the guts to come back here.

I bite the inside of my cheek and start to type.

I try to convey the way religion rooted itself so deeply into my mind and the minds of my family. I try to explain the feelings of inadequacy, the terror at realizing I couldn't stop looking at guys, the mix of panic and hope every time I was with Circus and pictured myself kissing him.

How desperately I'd wanted to be straight. How desperately I'd wanted to find a woman who'd consume me the way Circus did. How I'd thought maybe someone had come close. But I'd tried to force that friendship onto a path it couldn't manage, and I'd hurt her.

But it wasn't just her I hurt.

I lied to my family, my friends, myself.

I hurt Circus, which I don't think I'll ever get over.

But I'm trying.

I want to move on from all the negativity and start to do it right. To show my family that nothing has changed, and to show Circus that I'll be here always. Because the alternative isn't something I want to live through again.

I want people to know that if they're going through what I am, it can get better.

When I'm finally finished typing, I'm drained.

But I post it before I can talk myself out of it.

"There. Now everyone knows what I struggled through, and how you've always been there for me."

Circus smiles. "You mean you didn't tell everyone that we totally scammed them?"

"I just didn't think that approach would paint us in the best light for some reason. This way, it's closer to the truth anyway. Even when we were faking shit, it wasn't *fake*, you know?"

"Exactly."

I crawl across the couch to lie down and rest my head on his chest. "I'm tired."

"Want to go sleep?"

"It's like, three o'clock. And you don't have dark curtains."

"I hate sleeping in."

"Well, that doesn't help when a nap would come in handy."

When he laughs, I hear it deep in his chest. The sound is soothing and makes me feel all warm inside. He lifts his hand and starts to stroke his fingers through my hair, and my eyes fall closed. It's nice. Peaceful.

"In high school, would you ever, in a million years, have thought we'd end up like this?" I ask.

"Yes."

His certainty makes me sit up. "What?"

"I dunno." He looks a little uncomfortable, but

there's a cute smile trying to pull up his lips. "I used to think about it all the time. You coming out and telling me how you felt. Us doing college together or you taking over the diner while I worked out what to do with my life. Us traveling. Us here, just … living." He wrinkles his nose. "Now tell me, on a scale of one to never, how much should I have *not* just spilled all that?"

"It was ridiculously sappy. So I'd say a hard seven."

Circus groans and buries his face in one hand, but I hurry to pull it away. "Nope, not done trying to stuff my emotions back away."

I bark out a laugh. "Dude, I have literally cried all over you after sex. I don't think there's anything you could do or say at this point to top that."

"True. That was pretty embarrassing for you."

I twist his nipple, and he lets out a yelp. "You make me feel safe enough to be vulnerable."

"Oooh, that was a strong eight."

"And I think about you always."

"We're approaching a nine …"

"You make it easy to be myself."

"Abort, abort."

I shut him up with a kiss. "And I never want to know what it's like without you in my life again. You're easily the greatest person I've ever met, and you're pretty good in bed too."

He slumps. "You killed me with a ten."

"I'll give you tens every day."

He breathes out a laugh and runs his fingers down my cheek. "I was offered a movie role."

"What? That's—"

"Not what I want."

"But I thought …"

"Yeah, at one time it might have been right. But not anymore. I already messaged Preston to decline."

I glance at his phone. "How isn't he ringing nonstop by now?"

"I turned my phone off."

"You? Disconnected from technology?"

"I'm going to make an effort to be a little less intense about it. I mean, I have all the money I could ever need, and with you here, I don't know … I sort of want to do something else. Maybe. I'm not really sure yet, but I don't want to give it all up completely. I enjoy it. I just sort of want to get fulfillment from other areas too."

"That's amazing."

"Or stupid?"

"Nope. Just solidly amazing."

I'm sure some part of Circus is turning the movie thing down because of me, and maybe I should feel bad about that, but if he's looking to start life outside of the virtual one he's created for himself, I'm here for it.

I'll support him in any way he needs, and I know he'll do the same for me. He always has.

And that's why, even after only a few months back in each other's lives, I know I'll do whatever I can to make him happy.

We fit.

And we'll keep helping each other fight off our doubts and the dark thoughts that try to take over.

Because no matter what, I'm happier now than I've ever been in my life.

And I have a feeling the best hasn't even hit yet.

CHAPTER THIRTY FIVE
Circus

The Summer Nights Festival is easily my favorite Sunbury event. The warm night air smells like apples and peaches from the fruit stalls up and down O'Connell Road, and the strings of brightly colored bulbs hanging over the street wash everything in rainbow shades.

I turn from the window and look around at what, a couple of weeks ago, was an empty storefront and smile at how far it's come in the short time.

Arms circle my waist as Rowan presses a hard kiss just behind my ear.

He holds a churro up in front of me. "I bought you food."

"Mmm, sustenance."

"Enjoy the sugar while you can. Once the gym is ready, our eating plan starts."

Joke's on him. I'm looking forward to eating healthy.

And working out here.

We were lucky that Leon was able to squeeze in the shop before he's contracted to start the huge shopping complex construction in Port Welling. But some days I do feel bad because he's starting to look tired.

"Okay, plumbing should be fitted next week," Leon calls as he appears from out the back. "Then we've just got to tile and polish everything up and you should be good to go."

"I can't believe how quickly you did all this," Rowan says. Leon and I share a quick look. Money can make anything happen.

"The thing is, I've had an idea." I have to force the confession out because it isn't something I've even mentioned to Rowan yet.

"I don't like when you have ideas," Leon says.

I laugh and flip him off. "Too late for that, my friend. I've been talking to Joe from next door, and he's thinking of retiring soon. So ... I had the idea that maybe I could buy that shop, open up the wall between the two and ..." This is the part they better not fucking laugh at. But when I meet Rowan's eyes, in one look he reminds me that he'll support me with whatever. I clear my throat. "I want to start a daycare or kids' club or something so parents can work out whenever they want."

Leon sighs. "And by 'had an idea' you mean it's already in the works, isn't it?"

"Happening six months from now, yep."

"I guess I'll start drawing up plans." Leon takes out his measuring tape and moves toward the wall.

Rowan turns to me. "What brought this on?"

"Well ... I really like kids. And it's still a while before we even crack open *that* conversation, so finding a job where I got to work with them sounded like a good idea. There are some courses I'll take, and I'm going to deck that shop out like a kid's fever dream. It'll be—"

He laughs and presses his lips to mine. "Absolutely perfect."

He knows without me saying that this is another outlet where I'll be moving away from my virtual life some more. The psychologist I had an appointment with last week supports me wanting to keep that side of me alive but has encouraged I create balance. So that's what I'll do.

I don't want to miss my time with Rowan.

And while he runs classes and trains people, I'll be right next door helping kids finger-paint, or reading them books, or annihilating some preteens at one of the gaming consoles I'm going to have installed.

So maybe I don't have a complete plan yet, but the details will come. I mean, in just a few weeks we've already made Rowan's dreams come true.

People are in and out all night, taking in the gym and asking questions about the types of equipment and classes Rowan will have.

I leave him to it, happy to stand in the background, handing out flyers for discounts to anyone who walks in the doors.

Watching him, I can't remember a time I ever felt this happy.

And that knowledge always comes with a fresh tinge

of guilt. I'll never not miss my parents. But I also know that this, right here, is all they ever wanted for me. So while I let the guilt in for a little while, I don't let it drag down my mood.

Someone knocks into me from the side. "Oops, sorry, Circus," Brenda says, breathlessly. "I'm trying to get these up in all the shops for the festival, but I've just spent ten minutes arguing with that useless Eric Fletcher about the gay agenda and—" She cuts off. "Long story short, his flag is up, now I need to pop this one up before Rowan sees."

I almost laugh at the bunch of rainbow flags she's clutching. She hurries to the window, pins the flag up at an awkward angle, and then hurries off again. Brenda and Karl are still awkward around us, and still worried that we're going to hell, but they're trying to love us anyway.

Sometimes, like tonight, she swings *way* too hard to the supportive side.

"What was my mom doing?" Rowan asks. Apparently she's not the ninja master she thinks she is.

"The usual. Supporting her son, spreading the gay agenda ..."

"I don't want that up in the window. It's like ... I'm advertising or something. My business has nothing to do with me being gay."

He starts for the window, but I catch his shoulder. "Better leave it. Apparently we're not the only ones who've been attacked by rainbows."

"Do I want to know?"

I nod toward the door, and Rowan follows me out onto the street. Sure enough, in all the storefronts up and down the street are little rainbow flags.

He shakes his head. "Total overkill."

Laugher comes from behind us as Leon steps out of the gym. "You think this is overkill? You should see the diner."

"Oh God, no."

"It looks like a Pride parade threw up in there."

"Gross."

"Yeah, but the rainbow shake was delicious."

The disgusted look on Rowan's face makes me laugh.

"Excuse me, are you Leon Jefferies from LJ Construction?"

I look around for the voice and find a skinny guy staring straight at Leon.

"Yeah, that's me."

The ... kid? Maybe? I mean, he's small, but I don't *think* he's much younger than us, holds his hand out to Leon.

"I'm Auggie. I've submitted an application for the apprentice you're looking for, and since I drove up for the festival tonight, I thought I might introduce myself if I saw you."

The guy's trying so hard to be professional, but his

words just keep vomiting out of him.

"I mean, your whole story is impressive. No college, started the company from scratch and built it from the ground up. Now you have one of the biggest contracts this side of Portland ..." He laughs awkwardly. "Now it sounds like I've been stalking you. I haven't, so you know. But ... yikes, okay, that sounded *really* stalkerish." His face floods with a blush. "Oh, man, I really need to stop talking, don't I? Sorry, I just, sometimes I struggle to do that."

Leon seems confused as hell as he looks the guy up and down, and I know exactly what he's thinking. There's no way this guy could lift *one* brick let alone build anything.

Hiding a laugh, I hold a flyer out to the guy and cut him off just as he opens his mouth again. "We're opening in a month. You should stop by."

Apparently my offer is too much because he blinks in surprise and quickly takes the flyer before backing up. "Umm, yeah, thanks. Okay, that's all. Look out for my name. Or don't. I mean, just umm ... maybe I'll see you around. At work?" He gives a fake laugh. "Or not. Okay. Bye."

He turns and flees, and the second he's gone, Rowan can't hold back his laugh. "What the hell was that?"

"Enthusiasm?" I offer, because seeing how embarrassed he was makes me feel bad for him.

Leon stuffs both hands in his pockets. "That was

weird."

"I'll say." Rowan tugs me closer and presses a kiss to my hair. "I don't think I've ever heard someone talk that fast."

"Or prove so quickly that they are the complete opposite of what I'm looking for."

"You're mean," I tease.

Leon points down the road. "There's no way I'm putting up with that every day."

He has a fair point. The guy was a bit intense.

"Anyway, I'm off. With the town this full, there's gotta be good pickings at Ugly's later."

We say goodbye to Leon as he leaves, and I stand there, surrounded by Rowan's arms as we watch the families in the street.

"You know," Rowan says after a few moments of silence, deep voice tickling my ear. "You're right that we're not in a place to be having that conversation, not yet anyway. But ... I want it one day. A future with you. Kids with you. I want to give you the biggest family you ever dreamed of."

I can't stop my smile. "I want *five* kids."
"Sure."
"And three goats."
"Okay."
"Maybe a rooster, and some chickens."
"Circus ..."
"And a whole herd of alpaca."

His silent laugh hits my neck. "Why don't we start with one and go from there?"

"One Rowan."

"And one Circus."

Everything inside me settles. "That sounds like the perfect start to me."

EPILOGUE
ROWAN

Two Months Later

I've never seen Circus happier, which is bizarre considering the twenty-four hours we've just had.

After visiting his parents' graves yesterday and following it by having an awkward dinner with my family, by the time we got home, we were both feeling flat.

My parents are ... trying, I guess. Dad barely spoke, and Mom spent the whole time bringing up business. Either the gym, or the diner, or Circus's modeling.

It could have been worse.

The whole day is weighing on me, but Circus has already been out to collect the eggs from our chickens and is looking over the list for today's party.

Red, white, and blue decorations are everywhere.

"Happy Fourth of July," I say cautiously as I join him in the kitchen.

His smile splits his face. "Too much?"

"I think you hit too much about ten garlands of flags ago ..." At least. I can't see the ceiling through everything hanging from it. His long table has red, white, and blue flowers running down the middle, there are American flags hanging from the walls, and on the grass outside he's set out blankets and cushions around a fire pit. "I didn't know you were so patriotic."

His full lips turn into this cute little pout. "It's our first holiday together. I wanted it to be ... memorable."

God, he melts me. "I can safely say this is unforgettable." Circus lets me pull him closer, and I wrap my arms around his waist. "When did you do all this?"

"I've been up since five."

I laugh. "Why didn't you wake me?"

"Yesterday was a big day."

"For both of us," I point out. "It was your first time visiting them." He squirms a little in my arms. I'll never forget the pain on Circus's face. It took so much out of him to finally go out to the cemetery, and then to face my parents and play the role of perfect boyfriend seamlessly, I don't think I've ever been so impressed by him.

"I want to go more often. I think I felt guilty more than anything."

"We will." I kiss his hair. "Whenever you like."

"As much fun as it is to sit here and relive my grief, we also have a hell of a lot to do before everyone gets here."

"Okay, put me to work."

He thrusts a list at me. "Food. That's all you need to worry about. And Rowan?" He pins me with a serious look. "No pressure, but make sure it's perfect. This is the first time I've had anyone here, and I'm just a bit nervous."

"I got that impression." It's sweet though. Him wanting to impress his friends—*our* friends. And it feels oddly grown-up of us to be throwing a party in our home. "We don't need to talk about how much all this cost, do we?"

"Probably best not to. Especially if we factor in the fireworks."

"Fireworks?"

"It's the *Fourth* of *July*."

I drop my head onto his shoulder and muffle my laugh. "Never a dull moment with you."

"You're welcome."

And I wouldn't have it any other way. With Circus, it doesn't matter if we're on a day trip somewhere, or having a few nights in LA, or spending a lazy Sunday on the couch. He's my everything.

Coming back to Sunbury, I never imagined my life would turn out like this, let alone that Circus would be a part of it.

And while I'll always regret how I left and how long we spent apart, I know I wouldn't be here without it.

I'm also lucky enough to have the rest of our lives to make it up to Circus.

He deserves nothing less.

And for the first time ever, I can give him all of me.

Including the best Fourth of July he's ever had.

I grab the *Kiss the Cook* apron he bought me for my

birthday and point to the words. "Out of interest, should this be a general rule whenever someone enters the house?"

He smirks. "I wonder how red Tanner would go if we suggested it?"

"And how dead *I'd* be after Royce was finished with me?"

"New plan. I'll kiss you enough for everyone."

And he does. Slow and deep, and I return it just as lazily.

"Love you," I murmur against his lips. "Always have."

"And always will."

THANKS FOR READING!

To keep up to date with future releases, come join Saxon's Sweethearts.

www.facebook.com/groups/saxonssweethearts/

FAKE FRIENDS

HAVE YOU READ TOTAL FABRICATION?

Fake Boyfriends. Reality TV. What could go wrong?

When Jace and Blake are accepted onto Total Fabrication, it's supposed to be easy. Renovate a house, take out the win, walk away with the money. Reconstruction is what they do on the daily—even the reality TV aspect can't throw them.

But there's just one little problem.

Jace and Blake are the show's token gay couple ...

Who aren't actually a couple at all.

FAKE FRIENDS

Telling anyone they broke up is the blueprint for disaster, but with one poorly-timed video, two nosey contestants, and a shit ton of sexual tension, can they really keep up the illusion of the relationship they totally fabricated?

Or is it destined to the one thing they demolish and can't rebuild?

This short story is only available to newsletter subscribers so click below and join the gang!

www.subscribepage.com/totalfab

WANT MORE FROM SAXON JAMES?

Follow Saxon James on any of the platforms below.
www.facebook.com/thesaxonjames/
www.bookbub.com/profile/saxon-james
www.instagram.com/saxonjameswrites/

OTHER BOOKS BY SAXON JAMES
www.amazon.com/Saxon-James/e/B082TP7BR7

LOVE'S A GAMBLE SERIES:
Bet on Me
Calling Your Bluff
NEVER JUST FRIENDS SERIES:
Just Friends
Fake Friends
CU HOCKEY SERIES WITH EDEN FINLEY
Power Plays & Straight A's
Face Offs & Cheap Shots

And if you're after something a little sweeter, don't forget my YA pen name
S. M. James.
These books are chock full of adorable, flawed characters with big hearts.
www.amazon.com/S-M-James/e/B07DVH3TZQ

FAKE FRIENDS

ACKNOWLEDGEMENTS

As with any book, this one took a hell of a lot of people to make happen.

First, my cover designer Story Styling Cover Designs did a fantastic job on finding the perfect angst for the cover. Thanks to Sandra from One Love Editing for my amazing edits, and Karen Meeus, Louisa Masters, and Chelsea Bell for taking the time to beta read. They helped me make this book stronger than I could on my own.

Lori Parks, you were a gem as always with my proof read and I always appreciate how timely you are with your work.

Thanks to my formatter Rebecca Bosevski, for fixing this mess of a word doc and making it look ridiculously professional.

Eden Finley, your notes and ongoing commentary were fucking incredible, and thank you for letting me pick your brain while talking absolute smack at each other.

Amanda Johnson, your unwavering support and beautiful encouragement always give me the boost I need and I'm so grateful to be able to talk your ear off whenever I need to.

And of course, thanks to my fam bam. To my husband

who constantly frees up time for me to write, and to my kids whose neediness reminds me the real word exists.

SAXON JAMES

Printed in Great Britain
by Amazon